A SUITABLE WIFE

AWAY TO AFRICA
BOOK THREE

UNOMA NWANKWOR

KEVSTEL PUBLICATIONS

DEDICATION

I'm thankful to God from Whom the gift comes.

To Kevin, Fumnanya & Ugo
To my beloved mother, Amama
I miss you like crazy, and I love you. Always & Forever.

Lastly to my readers, thank you for rocking with me!

AUTHOR'S NOTE

Away to Africa is the second volume of my sweet romance collection, Afro Luv Bites.

Here, we follow the Kalu family. More specifically the three male cousins Arinze, Cheta & Jidenna. We first meet the family in New Year's Kiss which is a short prequel. Although you don't have to read that or book one (Rent A Bae) to enjoy this, but I'd recommend you do so for maximum enjoyment. A Suitable Wife is the final book in the series and is Jidenna & Zola's story.

A few things…

This book introduces the fictional town of Luxe Noir. It is a Black affluent town located on the outskirts of South Carolina. If you want more details about the town, click here. The town will now be a staple in the U.N. Universe.

Also, the meaning of all Igbo/Pidgin language is inferred in context. However, if you need translations, there is a glossary at the back of the book.

Lastly, don't forget to read the **Final Note.**

Happy Reading!

PS: In case you are wondering, the first volume of my sweet

romance collection is the Billionaire Pact and is available on all major online retailers.

Unoma

1

JIDENNA KALU

"Your mother is driving me crazy." Feeling the beginnings of a headache, I leaned back in my chair, interlocked my fingers behind my head, and lifted my tired eyes to the ceiling.

The chill in the room from the early, mid-February morning had been tempered by the warmth of the building. I let out a breath as my younger sister's lighthearted chuckle on the other end of the video call grated my nerves. For a few moments, the sound floated through my office at JDK Creative Studio. I let my gaze fixate on the abstract painting on the wall before returning my eyes to the screen of the 16-inch MacBook Pro.

The haven that was my studio had, in the past several weeks, become my hideout. Located in downtown Atlanta, the studio was nestled between a busy commercial area and a vibrant arts and culture hub. When I first found the space, I knew it was perfect. After I closed on the property, my contractors had the place transformed to my specifications in a little less than six months. I had been open for three years now.

The walls were painted a warm hue with a white-cloud sprayed ceiling and a mosaic of stones for the floor. There was a showroom, a classroom for private workshops, and a reception area on the first floor, and my personal studio plus two offices for my manager and I on the second.

"When you were inviting her aaaaaand grandma, for that matter, to come for a visit, did you think you were Superman?" my sister asked.

I could see that she was Facetiming me from her office. She was the part-time manager of my pride and joy, my gallery, JDK Art House in Enugu, Nigeria. Before I opened anything anywhere else in the world, I wanted my footprint in my ancestral home. My family had made a mark with Kalu International Inc., but I wanted to make my own.

I rubbed my hand over my low-cut hair. "No. But she made it sound like the trip here would be a fast one. Quick turnaround. Highest two weeks." That story had sounded too sweet, so I had gone to my dad. "I also told Papa to insist she reports back to Enugu in two weeks. I don't know how your father failed me."

"Why are they my parents when they're getting on your nerves? You should've called Chi. She can get Mama to do anything." My sister scanned a paper before putting a forkful of Jollof rice in her mouth.

Chinyere was our older sister, who recently relocated with my nephews to join her husband in Switzerland. She was still trying to settle down and I hadn't wanted to bother her. But apparently I should have.

My mother was supposed to be in America to shop for her upcoming birthday and wedding anniversary, which were on the same day. She didn't have to do that because she wasn't even going to lift a finger for either ceremony. My siblings and I had hired an event planner to coordinate everything – up to a personal stylist for wardrobe. I told her that, so she said what she knew would get me every time.

"I miss Uju *nwa m*." My mom knew when she brought up my nine-year-old daughter, she won almost all the time.

My mother, Nnenna Kalu, was my world, but she could be a little much. Imagine my shock when the plane landed on the private strip, and she was with my grandmother. My grandmother was in her eighties. What was she doing flying that distance? I was used to only dealing with her overbearing behavior when I visited Enugu.

"Grandma wasn't supposed to come." I sighed. "And then, your punk cousins act like they can't make time to help me entertain them."

"Nna, stop being dramatic." Referring to me by my nickname, Onyi waved me off. "They've only been there for five weeks." She chuckled again before continuing. "Nze and Cheta are busy. You know, the whole new wives and all."

Arinze or Nze, an actor, was our oldest cousin and had recently married Jasmine, who was a floral designer. My cousin, Cheta, who was a year older than I, had married Reign who owned her skincare line.

To be fair, our grandmother had already stayed a week in both my cousin's houses. She wanted them married and now they were. Now, she'd turned her attention to clocking their wives' wombs. I almost fell out when Cheta said he almost put our grandma out when he returned home one day and saw her hands on Reign's stomach.

"*E wo! Omalicha*, in due time I trust you and my grandson. Don't make me wait too long *o*. You know, *Chineke* can call me any time."

I narrated the story to Onyi who couldn't stop laughing. "Can you imagine grandma saying they needed to hurry up and have a child because God could call her home any time? The drama." I shook my head. "The next day, Cheta told me to come get her. Now, I only see Cheta and Reign for Sunday brunch."

"I'm surprised Cheta didn't pack her up that night. Anyway, he's her favorite, so I know he wouldn't have." Onyi wiped the corners of her eyes to stop her tears of laughter.

Cheta didn't. But everyone knew he didn't play when it came to Reign, so he made sure our grandmother knew that was unacceptable...in a calm manner. He didn't just erupt as he could have, and I was glad he applied wisdom. Although he needed to set boundaries, he also knew how the Kalu family dynamic worked. Having Reign be seen remotely as the reason he yelled at our grandmother would've made his wife everyone's target. Especially the women, because no circumstance would've justified disrespecting our grandmother.

"I love them, but I can't wait for this weekend when I put them back on that plane."

Onyi grunted. She lived in the Kalu compound, so they were back to being her problem. I needed a breather.

Glancing at the home screen of my cell phone, I mentally calculated how much time I had before I needed to leave for Uju's school to get there on time. My eyes darted to the picture on my desk of my daughter, who was the reason I drew breath. The reason for everything I did.

I frowned as I thought about how things were going with her lately. Apparently, I was to blame for her recent missteps. I was trying my best to rectify things, but it would help if I knew exactly what I had done wrong. And where it was hurting.

Part of my solution to the unknown problem was to spend more time with her. The problem was, I had contractual obligations I made before the recent issues with her started. I was glad to refund monies if I needed to, but my name and reputation were also at stake. So I was trying to strike a balance by adjusting my schedule. One of those adjustments included eating lunch with her at her school once a week. No matter how many accolades I acquired being a junk sculptor, nothing would make sense if I lost my daughter along the way.

"Okay sis, I gotta head out to your niece's school. What's going on?"

For the next several minutes, my sister, who I trusted with

every fiber of my being, updated me on what was happening at the gallery. My vision for the art gallery was for it to be an upscale, high-end, exhibition space that showcased and sold all kinds of fine art from around the continent. Over the years, with profits from my shares at Kalu International Inc. and my work, I had been able to acquire modern and historic paintings, sculptures, photographs, and other types of visual artwork. There was also a part of the gallery dedicated to my creations.

The three-story building was a sleek, modern masterpiece with a minimalistic design. I took extra care to make sure the place met international standards and my employees were well-versed in the artwork we displayed. For those looking for something a bit more private, there was an exclusive VIP viewing room for collectors. Additionally, we held various events such as artist talks, soirees, and exhibition openings to introduce new pieces of art and draw potential buyers.

My sister worked for the family business, but she was also my eyes and ears at the gallery. Every Tuesday, she worked out of her gallery office, making sure its operations were running as smoothly as my manager said. He and the rest of the staff reported to her.

"Nna, we got another call from the Global Connect folks. Are you sure you don't want to reconsider? Twenty-five million dollars is a lot of money."

I shook my head. "And you know my rule. Not to brag, but I don't need twenty-five million dollars. I might *want* it but not enough to go against my rule."

"I know, I know, but the Eze Nri collection will be an opportunity to showcase our culture, and—"

"Nah sis, you remember how long it took me to track down and acquire all five masks in that collection." I felt rage creeping up my spine. Rolling my shoulders, I let out a low breath, remembering my anger had nothing to do with my sister.

For decades, museums all over the world have held art stolen from Nigeria, most notably the Benin bronze masks. I was happy that in recent years, the social stigma associated with their illegal acquisition made it difficult to sell or display them.

The Eze Nri masks were different, however. They had been scattered throughout Nigeria and were traded, gifted, or simply misplaced. Crafted from wood or other components and adorned with beads and shells, they embodied aspects of Igbo culture, having been used by rulers of the ancient Nri Kingdom as symbols of their history.

I had acquired authentic tenth to fifteenth century masks belonging to these traditional rulers, and I had a strict rule about displaying ancient relics and artifacts in white-owned museums. Our art and history had been stolen and displayed in white museums for far too long. It was our turn to display our own.

The people at Global Connect were well meaning. They seemed to be devoted to the celebration of Black and African culture, and had been respectful in their requests to display my masks, but I wasn't budging from my policy.

"It's a no, sis. What else you got for me?"

"Well, your manager has secured all the locations for pop-ups during our upcoming tour. We're waiting on all the insurance paperwork and contracts from two more people."

Next, my manager joined the call and for the remaining time, I gave instructions on how I wanted things to go. I'd planned to be there for the tour, but now I wasn't sure of my availability. Presently I was focused on finishing the *Salvage Symphony* collection. It was a commission job for a Saudi Arabian museum. That and teaching the two classes on sculpting and art history at Morehouse College were my primary focus until the end of the school year. Teaching was another addition to my already busy schedule I'd made recently.

Checking the time again, I realized I was pushing it. I needed to head out. Giving final instructions and a promise to call my sister the next day, I disconnected the call.

Picking up my keys, I grabbed my jacket and left the office. After peeping my head in next door for a moment to check on my other manager, I descended the stairs and made my way to my car. I had a lunch date with the most important lady in my world.

~

Later that evening, I sat slouched in my chair with my head cradled in my hands. What was supposed to be a nice lunch with my child, morphed into an impromptu session with her teacher.

I couldn't believe the things I was hearing about my child. How we got here was still a mystery to me.

One minute, I was holding Uju in my arms, promising God I would take care of the gift He'd entrusted to me. And the next minute, I couldn't even get her to tell me what was wrong. She was fighting, throwing tantrums, and being downright disobedient. All in one day.

That didn't sound like my JuJu, and I wouldn't have believed it if I hadn't been shown the camera footage. I saw her progressively cross boundaries I had put in place. She was behaving in ways I never would have imagined my sweet JuJu could have. With my cousins, her nanny, and me raising her in the best way we knew how, I thought I had everything under control. But clearly I didn't.

I was back in my home, seated in the middle of two women who thought they had all the answers to Uju's unpredictable behavior. Thankfully, my mother and grandmother had waited until after dinner when Uju had gone to bed to air their views. As punishment, I'd seized her iPad and she was grounded from afterschool activities. But still, I needed to get to the root of the issue.

"Nna, I know you don't want to hear this, but since you're so against taking a wife, let her go back with us," my mother said.

She knew how much I despised the idea. She also knew I was at my wits end. I didn't want to make a wrong move with my baby all because of my feelings. "Mama, I can't be away from her for that long. I still have obligations here that I can't pick up and leave."

"Nna *nwa m*, that child needs a mother. I know you think you can do it on your own, but you cannot," my grandmother said.

Securing her scarf on her head, my mother continued. "My son, JuJu is nine. Soon she'll have her first period. Would you know what to do?"

"Eww, mama, don't say that." I furrowed my brows. Periods meant babies. Babies involved boys and I wasn't ready to think of my child like that.

But they were right. Uju was becoming a young woman. She needed a woman's influence, nurturing and guidance into womanhood. I couldn't give her that. At all. So much was said about the negative effects of women raising sons without a father in the home, but what happened to a father raising a daughter without a mother. Was I setting Uju up for problems in the future by her not having a mother figure in her life? My mother and grandmother were silent for a few minutes as they let the whole JuJu starting her period thing sink in. Were they right? Did I need to let her go back to Nigeria to live with them, among women?

I shook my head to get rid of the thought.

My grandmother chimed in again. "Nna, *o kwa* in four months, you will come home. I have some very pretty women from our church that you can marry. You don't even have to do that love thing you young people do. Just marry her, and she will take care of my great-granddaughter."

I ran my hand down my face, hiding my disgust. My grandmother was forever trying to arrange marriages for people. I couldn't even blame her. I faulted the women who actually appeared when she called herself holding auditions. It happened to Arinze. If Ifunanya, Arinze's sister, hadn't leaked the video of the woman my grandmother had him set up to meet on a visit home, he would've walked into that situation blind.

The favor of God was on Cheta because before grandma even had the chance to start meddling in his business, a social media scandal brought him and his wife, Reign, together. As the only single grandson left, it was now my turn, and Uju's disruptive behavior gave grandma the added incentive she needed.

"Jidenna, find a wife on your own, or let us help you. We can help you select a respectable Igbo woman."

My mother sounded like she was picking out a suit for me to wear. A wife was a life partner. Marriage was something I'd tried in the past. On the slim chance I wanted another wife, it should be someone I knew. Someone that would be suitable for my daughter and me. There was no need to argue the point though. I'd been in this spot for an hour, recycling the same solutions.

I made eye contact with my mother. "Mama…" Then I turned to my grandmother. "*Nne anyi ukwu*, I know you both want what's best for Uju and me. And I've heard you." I stood and stretched my body. "We won't find a solution tonight and I need to rest. I have meetings in the morning." I kissed their cheeks and headed toward the stairs.

I heard them both sigh then began to whisper their disappointment. With one foot on the bottom stair, I turned my body toward them. "If by the time I come home, I don't have a wife or a solution, I'll do whatever you want me to do." My declaration put a smile on both their faces. "*Ka chi fo.*" After bidding them good night in my native tongue, I continued my ascent up the stairs.

Walking down the hall to Uju's room, I leaned my head against her door and took a breath.

I need your help, oh Lord. What kind of promise had I just made to my mother and grandmother? They would never let me forget it, nor would they let me renege on it. Four months? What was I thinking? Where would I get a suitable wife in four months?

I entered my daughter's room, careful not to step on anything that would squeak. I put Uju's exposed leg under her duvet and pulled the covers up from her waist. Sitting on the edge of the bed, I touched her dark brown skin which smelled of baby powder with the added mango citrusy smell of the body mist from Reign. Her black hair, which was in what I learned was two strand twists was secured in a silk bonnet she'd also recently started wearing. Uju was my twin, but her mannerisms were the perfect mix of her late mother, Eno, and me.

It was in my junior year of college that I met Eno. Our… story was still hard to tell. The chemistry between us was instant and we quickly became friends. We loved each other, but at the time, loved our career paths more.

I fell in love with art when I took a class in high school in Enugu. After writing a paper on the Igbo Ukwu sculptures, I couldn't stop thinking about the ingenuity of my ancestors. Studying arts, however, was almost a taboo for Nigerian parents. So, I headed to Morehouse College like my cousins before me. I studied Mechanical Engineering, thinking I could add my skills to Kalu International Inc.'s luxury cars and buses business. By graduation, I knew I wasn't going to work for the family. I had attended an art history class for an elective and my passion was refueled. I gave my parents the degree, but a year later, I enrolled in a prestigious arts school in Cape Town, South Africa. I had my plans in South Africa and Eno had hers at the Culinary Institute in New York. I sighed thinking about our too-short time together. I had failed Eno in many ways; I couldn't risk failing our daughter too.

Kissing Uju on her forehead, I stood and left her room. As I was shutting the door, my eye caught her pink ballet shoes in the corner. Walking over to pick up the shoes, my mind traveled to her fine dance teacher, Zola Westbrook.

My lips moved up into a grin as I remembered the woman who came dangerously close to making me do what I promised myself I'd never do again. Open my heart up to another woman.

2

ZOLA WESTBROOK

I forced down another sigh. This one would've been heavier and more audible than the last, but Naomi Westbrook wasn't going for that. Not when she'd spent unbillable hours coaching and molding her seven children into proper, respectable citizens of society. The Westbrook name was synonymous with Black wealth and prestige, gained through hard work and passed down from generations.

"No child of mine will bring shame to the Westbrook name, or there will be consequences."

I could hear the threat of my youth as though it were yesterday. Whether she was serious or not, neither I, nor my siblings wanted to find out. Over the years, my siblings and I towed the line. Until a few years ago when I, the second to the last child, had become the prodigal one. That had to be the reason she was always on my case.

I leaned into the open refrigerator in the kitchen of my three-bedroom, luxury condo in the heart of Atlanta. Retrieving the berries I bought the day before, I walked to the sink. I looked into the stern eyes of my mother through the propped up iPad.

"Mom, I can't make it though."

"Yes, you can, and you will," she asserted, looking up from some document her assistant, Ellie, handed her. Her reading glasses were perched perfectly on her nose.

I peered into the screen next to the sink. She seemed to be in her home office at our family home in Luxe Noir. All the major annual functions she hosted were drawing near and she was in "go" mode. But I didn't have to "go" with her. But that was a sentiment neither, I nor my siblings dared voice.

I smiled thinking about my family. My siblings and I grew up in Luxe Noir. We lived busy lives, but remained close. Luxe Noir was made up of a small town, Luxe Noir Bay, and a connecting island, Luxe Noir Island, near the outskirts of South Carolina. One of the few remaining original, historic settlements of formerly enslaved African people, the township, with less than nineteen thousand residents, was notorious for the many festivals it held throughout the year.

My mother chaired most of them and everything she was involved in, so were we. Which was the reason she couldn't resist waking me up at the crack of dawn on a Saturday morning. Technically, it wasn't *the* crack of dawn, but it was early for me. I didn't get back from the dance studio, Leap & Twirl, until almost midnight. I promised myself I wouldn't get up until nine a.m., but alas, my mother had other plans at seven.

Securing the tie on my robe, I poured a little baking soda on my berries and washed them. I would've loved a big breakfast of ackee and saltfish this morning, but my bestie, Tessa Ezra, was arriving in two hours and we had the whole weekend planned. So, oatmeal it was. I grabbed the cutting board and began to slice strawberries, blueberries, and bananas.

"Mom, I have a dance performance I need to be preparing for. I really can't make it."

"Aren't you supposed to be the owner of that place? Let the other teachers prepare the children."

"I'm the director, not the owner."

That was a half-truth. One, because I rarely saw Mrs. Donovan, the owner, and two, I signed on as the director of Leap & Twirl Dance Studio with a three-year option to buy. The studio which enrolled girls from ages four to twenty-five, was rich in Black history and had been in the community for years. My teachers and I taught ballet, hip hop, contemporary, African dance, and acrobatics. We also held private classes and took part in competitions and performances. Its smooth operation lay in my hands and while I loved what I did, I still hadn't decided if I wanted to own it yet. I had to make that decision soon.

"Mommy…"

"Don't whine. And don't tell me *that* is breakfast?" My mother scrunched her nose.

I remained silent, choosing to close my eyes to prevent her from seeing them roll.

"You need to come home, so you can eat better."

It had only been a month that I hadn't been home, but hearing it from my mother, I was the runaway child. Since my older siblings lived in other parts of the United States and abroad, they were off the hook from being badgered about coming home. I happened to live in Atlanta, the closest, so was expected to be home every weekend.

The affluent Black community of Luxe Noir was filled with people whose material wealth was a source of pride and gave them the perceived right to place judgment on anyone who painted the town in a bad light. As a divorced Westbrook, I felt the stares and heard the whispers every time I stepped out of the house. After months of this treatment, I found myself beginning to dread each visit home and had to discipline myself to manage the exposure in small doses.

"I eat okay right where I am."

This is why I moved away, but not far enough.

"Then you know Saturdays are for ackee, porridge, or fritters…not…what is that?"

"It's an oatmeal bowl and very nutritious."

My mom was a second-generation Jamaican American married to a Black American man. Although neither she nor my grandmother ever lived in Jamaica, they held on to their culture and passed it down to my siblings and I. Ackee and saltfish were our Saturday morning jam.

"I'll eat porridge next Saturday. I promise," I said, trying hard to stifle my laughter.

"Keep laughing, young lady," my mother warned.

"Back to the issue, can't you get Zuri to do it with you?" I asked.

My younger sister was the poster child for the "princess of old money." She had two degrees she might never use, a condo in one of the most expensive complexes in Luxe Noir, had a personal trainer, and shopper, and was always jet setting with the family's jet. She loved those kinds of things.

"She'll be in Rhode Island with Ted's family."

I palmed my forehead. Lil' Sis was getting married next year, and I honestly couldn't wait, as my sister was head over heels for her man. The only hiccup was that these types of events gave my mother the perfect opportunity to accidentally place men in my path. My dad heard me complaining about it when I went home the last time. He promised to bring his wife to order. But I wasn't so sure. Richard Westbrook might be the feared and respected, multi-million-dollar head honcho at Westbrook Equity Group, but we all knew who he answered to.

"Okay, how about—"

"Zola, I already promised no incidental meetings if that is what you're afraid of. What I will not do is host the Divine Soirée without my daughter."

What she really wanted to say was without my *single* daughter. The Divine Soirée was Luxe Noir's version of a cotillion. Unlike other more traditional cotillions, the community held it in conjunction with The Gathering Place, which was the local church. The event also included some African elements in honor of the town's original residents.

There were four things my mother didn't play about. The Lord, her family, her status, and Luxe Noir. Sometimes I wasn't sure which order they came in, but it was those four things.

Not willing to argue any further, I acquiesced. "Okay, I'll be there." It wasn't for several weeks anyway, so why argue?

For the next couple of minutes, I assembled my breakfast, made my matcha latte, and settled on the kitchen island to eat while still talking to my mother. We discussed a wide range of topics from her foundation to my dad's business, to her friends whose kids were getting married, or their husbands who were suspected of cheating on them. Normal small-town gossip sprinkled with my life and gossip about my siblings.

Although my mother didn't spare discipline while we were growing up, she was the most loving and caring woman I knew. And we knew she was proud. I had mixed feelings about the "strong" Black woman adjective, but my mom was a superhero and I respected her for it. No matter how much we disagreed sometimes.

Naomi Westbrook wasn't a woman who married into money and lived in the affluence of Luxe Noir Bay. She was the second daughter of Lottie and Bryon Reid of Stamford, Connecticut, the owners of the multimillion-dollar Reid Textile Enterprise. She came from generational wealth. I guess money found money because she and my dad met at the University of Connecticut. He was in his final year of a master's program while she was in the senior year of her undergrad program.

Over the years, while my dad returned home to Luxe Noir to work in the family business, my mom went on to law school and became one of the most respected Black family lawyers in Connecticut before moving after they were married. No matter what, I couldn't remember a time when my mother didn't put her family before all else while still stepping on folks' necks in the courtroom.

My mother diverted her eyes briefly. "Darling, Ellie sent me another florist."

Her long-time decorator who also supplied her flowers moved to California to be with her family. Although she recommended a new decorator that worked out, the floral part of the relationship had my mother displeased. This was the third one she was interviewing.

"If that one doesn't work out, I have someone for you." My sorta friend, Jasmine Kalu, owner of Luxe Petals, was a master at floral decor. Although she lived in Atlanta, I was sure she wouldn't have a problem traveling for business.

"Speaking of, I'd love for you to invite your new famous friends for the annual gala later this year."

The tug in my heart at my mother's statement caused me to wince. That was a topic I didn't like to talk about. Especially since I'd obviously ranked myself higher in their lives than I was. Maybe not them, but him. Shaking my head to rid myself of the bitter memories, I nodded. I didn't want to talk about it.

"I'll call you back and we'll talk about it."

"No Mom, that's okay. Handle your rich people's business, I have to get ready. Tessa will be here soon."

"Stop being smart, little girl. Anyway, say hello to my dear Tessa."

A few laughs and I love you's later, we disconnected the call.

Tessa, my best friend for over twenty years, had recently returned to Luxe Noir after her mother took ill. After our high school graduation, we'd both left the small town to see what the rest of the world had to offer. We had been on trips with our parents, but we wanted to do so on our own. So, we traveled to Europe and Africa for a year before we returned to the States to continue with our education. I couldn't wait to see her.

Your order has shipped.

I glanced at the text notification I received from BGE. My skincare products were low, and I needed to restock them. Although I could walk into the Body Glow Essentials store, owned by Reign Kalu, I'd been trying to keep my distance from that gang. By gang I meant Jasmine, Reign, and their Nigerian-American husbands, Arinze, and Cheta, but more especially their husbands' cousin, Jidenna Kalu. By the looks of things, he was keeping his distance from me too. I hadn't seen his daughter, Uju, in my dance class for two weeks.

~

"Listen to this part."

Opening my Kindle, I went to my bookmarked location. I felt Tessa's heated gaze on me, but I didn't care. S.D Harris was my shero of all sheroes and she was in Atlanta. I'd been following the *New York Times* bestselling, romantic suspense author for several years. Tessa was the one that put me on to her, but now my obsession with S. D Harris's mind surpassed hers. Once I found out she was coming to Atlanta to sign her latest book, *Betrayal in the Shadows*, I got us tickets immediately. She hissed and shoved another undeserving dress to the side. She was upset that she couldn't find the dress she wanted in Nordstrom after being promised it was in the store.

"Stop stressing. You want to stand out anyway. I know of these new, well new-to-me African designers. They have a pop-up shop in Lennox." I swiped to the calendar app on my phone. "They're leaving next week. So, we can check there after the signing. You'll find something."

With her hands balanced on her hips, Tessa sized me up. We were the same age, but different in everything else, weight and height. I knew I looked good, but her hips were curvier and matched her five-three frame better. I was three inches taller and would love a little more meat. We both had sun kissed, deep brown skin.

"You've been throwing the word "African" around a lot, and what do you mean *you* will? What about you?"

"The first part, I won't dignify. The second part, *I'm* not going on a blind date. Stop trying to set me up."

"You lie. I've been walking the stark halls of Luxe General Hospital all week. I didn't fly all this way not to hear the latest on your "African studies." And you most certainly are going on a blind date."

I laughed at her referring to Jidenna as "African studies," but still ignored her as she shoved two more dresses to the side. "It's a little over an hour flight, so I don't know how that qualifies as 'all this way'. Tell me, what's going on at LGH?"

My girl was making serious bank at Luxe General Hospital as an anesthesiologist.

She shook her head. "Nope, we're talking about you." She slumped her shoulders for dramatic effect and blew at a loose braid that fell from her bun. "I set this date up weeks ago and I don't wanna hear it."

"What is it with you and my mother trying to force me to go places I have no desire to be?"

Tessa chuckled. "That's because me and Auntie MiMi know what's up. We're forever trying to get you together." She placed her hand on my shoulder. "Do better, Zee. Do better."

I shrugged her off. "Girl, if you don't take your hand off me acting like Mr. Miyagi…"

"Miyagi, Oprah, Brené Brown, I'll be anyone I have to be to help you make better choices."

Before I could proffer my response, my alarm blared. Quickly silencing it, I pulled Tessa's arm until we were out of the store. The Black-owned, independent bookstore where the signing was taking place was about a ten-minute walk on this shopping strip and my alarm that was thirty minutes ahead said it was time to head there.

An hour and a few minutes later, I joined the applause in the room as S.D Harris lifted her eyes. The middle-aged, Black woman transported us to another world as she read from her latest book. My heart thumped in my chest as the story reached its climax, when the heroine discovered the man she'd come to trust had betrayed her.

It reminded me of Jidenna. He was sweet, but when he ghosted me, I knew for a fact he was simply rude. He was probably one of those guys who played with women's emotions for sport.

I replaced my disdain with a smile as I dragged Tessa up to get into the line for the Meet and Greet portion of the event. I balanced the six books I'd bought in my arms.

Tessa leaned in. "Don't you have all these books in eBook?"

"Your point?"

Shaking her head, my bestie took some of the books from me. "At least you don't do drugs, so I should be grateful."

"You see, count your blessings." Once I got the books signed, we were off to dinner and back to my place.

Hours later, Tessa and I were seated in the living room of my condo. The subtle blue and grey decor usually provided a feeling of peace, but right now her intense gaze made it hard to relax. I was on the plush carpet with my back against an accent chair, staring idly at the gorgeous view of Atlanta's skyline that the huge windows provided. Finally, I turned my gaze towards her. With some popcorn suspended midair on the way to her mouth, Tessa's brows dipped. This was the exact reason I didn't want to talk about Jidenna. But after she endured me fan girling over my favorite author for about forty-five minutes longer than planned, which ultimately led to us being late for dinner and our reservation almost being cancelled, she deserved to have her curiosity about Jidenna satisfied. Being away and dealing with her mother, it seemed trite for me to burden her with updates on such a non-issue.

After we ate, the Ziedu Fashions pop-up shop had shut down for the day. That meant both of us had to get up earlier than we'd planned tomorrow to get there and have brunch before taking her to the airport. She had to be in surgery early Monday morning.

I briefly ran over the minimal history of me and Jidenna's relationship, as if Tessa didn't already know. When Jidenna asked me to go with him to the Morehouse charity gala that he and his cousins went to every year, I agreed. He gave this story about not wanting to go alone and how this could be my repayment for him fixing my tire some days before. I'd insisted on owing him a favor for it. I didn't think it through because I knew nothing about the man other than he was my student's father and of course, he was fine on steroids. I allowed my mind a few moments to relish in the memory of him.

Jidenna's deep dark skin was smooth and there wasn't a blemish in sight. He towered over me. If I was to guess, 6 feet 4 inches. His voice was a deep rasp that I'm not ashamed to admit sent my heart racing. It was rich and smooth, the kind of voice that made you want to listen to him speak for hours on end. He had chiseled cheekbones and a strong jawline, but when he looked at me with those piercing brown eyes, every thought in my head came grinding to a halt. He carried his lean frame like a cheetah, moving with an effortless grace that made everything else around him look clumsy and awkward.

After the gala, I also showed up at his cousin's NBA championship parade. Then his family, mine, and the media began to speculate. I was used to the press, but not like that. Jidenna's older cousins, Arinze and Cheta, were an actor and an NBA player, respectively. The press couldn't get enough of them and were always dragging them over something. Jidenna, although relatively quiet, was also a well-known sculptor. After some research, I found out that his *Rustic Glam* and *Reclaimed Beauty* collections were the talk of the high-class art community a few years ago.

However, I was only at the parade because of Reign. At the time, she and her man were on the outs, and she needed a wing woman. She, I and Jasmine all had our businesses in Azili Plaza. The studio, however, was on the opposite end so I didn't see them often, but we had a good rapport.

"Earth to Zee. Earth to Zee. Again, you're telling me that in eight whole months, you haven't seen him?"

"No, I've seen him, but he doesn't say more than three phrases to me when he picks his daughter up from dance class. 'Hi, Thank You. Bye.' Almost like we didn't vibe on the two occasions we did see each other."

"Aww baby, are you feeling this man? You're all whiny."

I shrugged and picked up my glass of wine. "I guess more than anything, I want to know why…" That was a boldface lie because I was feeling him. Something serious. I'd like to know why but I'd stopped losing sleep over it. The night of the gala was perfect. We vibed, talked, danced. At one point during the evening, he'd gone to a secluded area to call the nanny to check on his daughter. I walked up behind him, and the DJ happened to start playing, "The Best Part" by H.E.R ft. Daniel Caesar. We stood there in a trance. I could feel the moment his soft lips were making their descent on mine. Because…whew! When they landed and he began to explore my insides, it was as though we were ascending to heaven.

The day of the parade, even though I wasn't there with him, when the crowd started pushing and getting rowdy, the way he grabbed his daughter and me…no one had protected me like that except my dad and brothers. So why would he ghost me?

"Girl, forget him. We're going to get you a man."

I chuckled. "Please, we're not making that a mission." Picking up the remote, I skipped to the next song. Glancing over to her, I asked, "What about you? Don't you need one?"

"Not need, but want. 'Cause honey, those designers' bags and shoes aren't doing anything for me at night." Tessa winked and shrugged. Although she tried to hide it, I saw the pain in her eyes. Both our parents have been married a long time and my girl wanted her happily-ever-after. I'd had it and it wasn't so great, but I wouldn't diminish her dream.

"But you know how it is, let a man find out I make three to four hundred thousand a year and suddenly I can't let them lead." She took another sip from her glass.

My friend was speaking pure facts. I'd seen her date a few men who suddenly started acting insecure.

"Man, I have to give *you* gas money. Lead me, to where?" She rolled her eyes.

I collapsed to my side when she said that, holding my chest. She had no sense whatsoever. Wiping the tear from my eye, I struggled to gather my thoughts.

"Don…don't worry about it. I'm certain this is your year. Keep focusing on you and watch God send you the man you deserve."

Tessa nodded. "Thanks, sis. I'll drink to that."

Surprisingly enough, once I was tucked into my bed, my mind didn't wander to Jidenna, but to the spawn of the enemy that I was married to for two years. Caleb Sterling. That was the choice Tessa and my mom should have made sure I didn't make. But no, she was a proud mother of the bride while Tessa cheered me on.

I turned over. I wasn't willing to let a situation I'd left four years ago deprive me of sleep. I'd done that for too many nights. I fluffed my pillow and closed my eyes. Now, my brain decided to entertain thoughts of another man I wanted to forget. For Jidenna though, my feelings were so much more complicated.

3

JIDENNA

onely and neglected.

Those words seared the middle of my chest like a white-hot blade, leaving me speechless. Two weeks after my meeting with my daughter's teacher, Uju's school counselor asked that we meet. My daughter had finally opened up to her, not a lot I was cautioned, but some. When those words were given to me as a summary, I took it hard.

I took the blame.

Nothing came before my daughter. I'd thought I'd done a pretty good job of making sure she understood that fact. But over the past several months, as I watched her move around the house with a pout and dark eyes marred with sadness, it seemed like she was challenging that very belief...

But neglected?

Lonely?

Okay, maybe I got the lonely part. Apart from two girls I knew were her friends from school, Uju had no playmate at home. I wondered if all only children felt that way, or was there something I wasn't doing right?

Neglect though? That was hard. I made sure she was

surrounded by family and had everything she wanted. My daughter was the reason I existed—that I got out of bed every morning and worked so hard. I loved her more than anything in this world and would protect her with my life. But her truth was her truth and I needed to figure out how to change that immediately. My thoughts went back to my conversation with my grandmother and mother. Was Uju feeling neglected because she didn't have a mother? Was this truly my fault? I would never want to send my daughter to Nigeria, but if that was best, did I need to just let go and send her? My child's mental and emotional well-being was at stake.

My thumbs tapped nervously against the steering wheel, the thump of each beat echoing through the car. The soulful melody of "Warm Embrace" by CalledOut Music was supposed to calm me down, but it wasn't working now. Every time I looked at the clock, I felt like I lagged further behind. The GPS put my arrival time to Leap & Twirl Dance Studio at fifteen minutes.

Late.

Fifteen minutes late.

My heart sank.

Uju, alone at the studio when everyone else had probably left would no doubt fuel the fire of her narrative. Once Eva, Uju's nanny, called to inform me of her family emergency, I ended the call with Ziedu Fashion's Marketing Director and hopped in my car. Although I was on the other side of town, between me and my cousins, I was still the closest to the studio.

I'd called to let the studio know I was running behind, all the while praying Zola wasn't the one who answered the phone. Thankfully, she wasn't. I slammed my palm against the wheel and glared at the car ahead. My built-up frustration threatened to spill over when I saw some space open ahead and the driver refused to take advantage of it. With a quick swerve to the right, I took the exit ramp to the studio in the distance. After a few more miles, I turned in.

Over the past several months, my cousins had teased me relentlessly for the route I'd taken with the brown-skinned beauty. No matter what they said, I knew my weaknesses. With Zola, I'd been dangerously close to dismantling the barricade around my heart I'd carefully crafted over the years.

That evening about eight months ago, in her presence, I felt my throat constrict, my heart race, and the hairs on the back of my neck stand. Suddenly, I was exposed and fragile…vulnerable, an emotion I'd banished to the recesses of my mind. When my lips captured hers in a moment of raw passion, I felt her melt into me. My overprotective streak took over. I wrapped my arm around her waist, clinging to her for my next breath while my fingers threaded her hair and tugged, claiming ownership of her and the moment, and eliciting a moan that still haunted my daydreams.

One date and Zola Westbrook had been able to put a dent in the wall I'd spent several years constructing to protect my heart. Why would I, in my right mind, give her the opportunity to annihilate it completely? So yes, I'd avoided her.

Uju had class on Wednesdays and Fridays in the evenings. Her nanny was mostly available to take her and pick her up. On the rare occasion that I had to, a quick "hello," "thank you" and "have a great night" always sufficed. I wasn't oblivious to the curiosity in her eyes. I felt terrible for not giving her what I was sure she wanted.

An explanation.

But not terrible enough to indulge her. Especially with everything else I had going on. With my mother and grandmother safely back in Enugu and the semester slowly ending, I was planning on taking Uju on a mini vacation. Just the two of us. I still had obligations I hadn't met, new commission deals and speaking requests awaiting my decision, and a mini, solo US tour with my popular collection pieces. For now, I didn't have time for any emotional entanglements with Zola. Not even a simple explanation.

After pulling into the parking space in front of the building, I jogged to the entrance. A lady I knew as an assistant walked up to let me in.

"Hey, Mr. Kalu. She's in the back with Miss Zola," she said.

I had two options—be a coward and ask her to get Uju for me, or get her myself. I knew exactly where they'd be. Despite my resolve about Zola, my brain didn't refrain from pushing her to the forefront of my mind at various times of the day. I wanted to lay eyes on her, so I opted for option two.

"Thanks. I apologize again for being late. I'll head back."

After she acknowledged me with a smile that turned her cheeks tomato red, I made my way to the back of the studio. I was dressed down today in dark jeans and graphic print waffle polo, and my matching Hermes sneakers were silent on the vinyl floors as I journeyed down the hall. Hearing voices, my steps faltered, then stopped.

"Now everyone thinks I'm bad for saying what I feel," Uju said, her voice unsteady.

I wanted to go in and reassure her, but I wanted to hear what she had to say. The fact that she seemed to be talking to everyone except me had my stomach in knots.

"Did your daddy say that?" Zola asked.

"No, my daddy loves me, but I didn't tell him. He draws a lot, and I don't like to bother him. I love to dance, and I'll be mad if someone stopped me while I was doing it."

Zola laughed. A soothing sensation crept up my spine.

"It's not the same thing, JuJu. Your daddy is the parent. It's not your job to make those kinds of decisions. It's unfair to him. If he doesn't know how you feel, he can't help you."

"But I don't feel like this all the time."

"Will you promise to talk to your dad, so you feel like this none of the time?"

"Yes. But will you please put me back in lead for the performance?"

Zola chuckled.

There goes that melodic sound again.

"Well, in your category, you are one of my best dancers. But you were gone for two weeks, so I had to put Asia in the lead position. Let's see how it goes."

"But pleeaaaaseee." Uju sighed.

"What did we discuss about whining and taking responsibility?"

"Actions have consequences and taking responsibility for them is showing I'm a big girl."

"Good. You were bad in school, so your daddy grounded you and as such, you lost your place in the performance…"

"I accept responsibility and the con—"

"Consequences. Good."

Through the reflection, I watched Zola tweak Uju's nose, causing her to giggle. When Uju flung her arms around Zola's neck, a feeling of utter satisfaction and ease settled in my gut. What it meant…I wasn't willing to dissect or verbalize. Not even to myself. I stepped out of the shadows, my heart pounding in my chest as I slowly released a long breath making my presence known.

"Good evening, Daddy," Uju jumped down from the table she'd been sitting on and scurried towards me.

I swooped her up, and we did our secret handshake before I planted a kiss on her forehead. Putting Uju down, I apologized for being late and asked her to go get her things. As soon as we were alone, Zola's gaze locked onto mine like a vice. The stare of her dark brown orbs was so potent that I could feel it searing into my skin. Blinking wasn't even an option – it was as though an invisible force held my eyelids open so I couldn't break our connection.

Despite the cool February weather, perspiration formed on

my forehead. The anger in her eyes also held a glimmer of hurt and disappointment. That's what propelled me to swallow the clog in my throat and step forward. She leaned on her desk with her arms across her chest and her legs crossed at the ankles. The closed stance wouldn't stop me though. As I got closer, she took flight to the back of her desk.

Clearing her throat, she lifted her eyes briefly. "Anna at the front desk can help you check Uju out."

I didn't expect her to berate me for being late because this was the first and only time. However, now, I had other things that held my focus. Like her shaky fingers, as she packed up the papers and laptop on her desk and stuffed them into her portfolio. Her clearing her throat over and over, as though she had a stubborn bone lodged in it. Her forced preoccupation gave me time to study her.

Her fine, jet-black hair bounced against her shoulders. There were some loose strands I desperately wanted to fix. The sexy, delicate, vanilla scent of her perfume mixed with the perspiration from her dancing wafted up my nose, driving me close to the edge. Zola had on a grey and black Nike set – black leggings with a grey, cropped-top hoodie. She completed the look with diamond studs in her ear, an Apple watch, and black Nikes. I was so caught up examining the way her buttocks shaped those leggings that I didn't realize when her desk became bare. What I did see when she lifted her phone was that she'd ordered an Uber.

"Is there something I can do for you, Mr. Kalu?" she asked, not caring to camouflage her irritation.

"What happened to your car?"

It might not feel like it to her, but nothing about our situation, or lack thereof, had anything to do with her. But right now, anything I wanted to say gave way to ensuring her safety. My eyes darted to my watch. It was almost eight thirty in the evening. Strange cars at any time were a no go for me. But this late? Nah. She was going to have to be angrier with me than she already was, but she wasn't getting in an Uber. Not happening.

I knew she lived in Buckhead, but I wasn't exactly sure where. My home in Alpharetta was no more than forty-five minutes from the area. I was taking her home. Either I was, or she had to call a family member or boyfriend.

Boyfriend.

The word fueled my unease.

"None of your business. If there's nothing—"

She tried to walk past me, but I grabbed her arm. The grip wasn't aggressive, but enough to hold her in place. "Anything you think about me, I deserve, but you're not getting in an Uber at this hour."

Our eyes locked. I was determined and I could tell she understood it would be a waste of time to try and fight me.

She rolled her eyes. "Mr. Kalu, I'm capable of taking care of myself. If you'll move, we can all end this long night."

This was the second time she'd used my formal title. Cute, but I drew her closer to me. "I get you're mad, and I want to explain if you let me."

How am I going to explain I'm feeling you, but don't want to put myself out there again? With other ladies, it's easier to satisfy my needs and keep it moving, but with you I want to be gentle. Savor everything about you until we let our human desires lead us to an explosive climax we won't want to come down from.

Nope, there was no way I could tell her all that, so I had to look for another explanation if she'd let me give her one.

"It's no longer required. Can we go now?"

"I'm sorry."

She sneered. "Whatever...let's go."

My response to her sass was halted when the lady I saw at the door entered with Uju. After explaining something about their security system shut down procedure, she said her boyfriend was outside. Uju ran up and placed her hand in Zola's outstretched one. From the drop of her shoulder, I could tell Uju provided her an escape from our conversation. I thumbed my nose and followed them out.

I heard my daughter's voice, but what she was saying to Zola lost out to my focus on the sway of her hips. Was this what she wore every day? My chest tightened. I had no right to even think that. Didn't even know if she had a man. One thing I did know was she shouldn't be entering any stranger's car dressed like that.

A few minutes later, Uju was tucked safely in the back seat while I stared Zola down. The first Uber canceled the trip and now her phone was in my hand, above her head because despite what I said, she was about to order another one.

"Mr. Kalu, give me my phone," she said, her voice terse, laced with irritation and exhaustion. "I'm tired and I wanna get home."

"One, stop calling me that and two, we would've been halfway there by now." I placed the phone in my pocket.

"I thought your cousin was the crazy one. I didn't peg you for—"

She was referring to Cheta. "He might be older, but I taught him everything he knows." I winked at her, and she sucked her teeth.

"Come on." I opened the car door and she reluctantly got in.

When I tried to fasten her seat belt, she swatted my hand. Chuckling, I let her be. Shutting the door, I walked over to the driver's side of my Genesis GV80. Handing my phone over, I instructed her to put her address in my GPS. Looking back, I saw Uju was slouched in slumber. Her headphones were still over her ears. Adjusting her neck, but leaving the headphones on, I caressed her face before settling down in my seat.

"Do you need to stop to get something to eat?"

With annoyance on her face, Zola ignored me and typed away on her phone with a ferocity and speed that seemed impossible. Her face contorted into scowls as she sent her messages, alternately hissing and rolling her eyes in agitation.

"Is this phone gonna be a problem between us?" I glanced at her just in time to see her raise her brow and tighten her nose in disdain. "Who is that anyway?"

"There's no us and mind your business," she snapped.

I suppressed a smirk. "For the next several minutes, you *are* my business. So again, do we need to stop and get you something to eat?"

Her eyes widened in anger. "I'm fine, Mr. Kalu. You insisted on kidnapping me, so take me home already." Her words were filled with contempt, her mistrust in me evident.

I clenched my jaw and tightened my fist around the steering wheel. "It's Jidenna." I messed up, so her anger was warranted, but it didn't make it any easier to take.

"Since I don't know anything about you except that you're my student's father, the formality is necessary."

Her words cut into me, and though they were right, they still stung. At the end of the Morehouse gala, we both decided we weren't ready to end the night. I'd enjoyed the way her velvety voice wrapped me in a cozy blanket and calmed the chaos that sometimes overtook my mind. So when she suggested coffee at a twenty-four-hour bookshop that served the best pastries and beverages – her words – I agreed. Zola had done most of the talking while reading parts of some of her favorite mystery books to me. I didn't offer up any details my Wikipedia page didn't already have. I might not have shared much but from our conversation, it was clear we had a lot in common. We had similar tastes in music, arts, and a healthy appreciation of sports. Instead of nights on the town, we preferred to stay at home watching movies or playing board games.

"We have to rectify that," I said.

"I'll pass."

"What are you doing tomorrow? Let me apologize again this time with an explanation."

"Again, I'll pass and none of your business. But since you won't let me be, I'm going home."

I remembered her telling me that she was from a town in South Carolina. The way she described the place – a mainland and island connected by a bridge – intrigued me, and sounded like parts of Lagos. Although her hometown was way smaller.

About half an hour later, I parked in front of her gated condominium building. I was pleasantly surprised when she let me open the car door. A part of me shouldn't have been. From her background and her general manner, I was positive chivalry was expected. In silence, I walked her to the double door entrance. I would've gone all the way to her front door, but my baby was asleep in the car.

"When do you get back?"

"I guess I need a t-shirt or a sign to wear on my forehead," she said, balancing her portfolio on her forearm.

"Why?"

She placed her hand on the door, but I pulled it open.

"Because I'm tired of telling you that nothing that concerns me is your business." She walked into the building.

This time I let her go. Crazy, but my body reacted with excitement at her outbursts, sending a wave of arousal through me. Her fight only served to fuel the fierce, raw, undeniable pull between us. Smirking, I tracked the sway of her hips as she marched through the well-lit lobby, heading for the elevators.

"Text me when you get into your apartment."

Not bothering to look at me, she shook her head and got into the elevator. Another grin of amusement crossed my face. Zola had no idea of the dark layers that were buried deep beneath the surface. Pain, agony, guilt, and regret that nearly cost me my daughter when she was a baby. I didn't think she could handle it quite frankly. Another reason I'd stayed away.

～

I was a man with single-minded determination some labelled as madness. I didn't move without a goal—that was a waste of energy. Reconnecting with Zola last night was dangerous, and wasn't in my best interest or hers. She made me feel things I wasn't prepared for again. I wasn't one of those men that feared love as mine ran deep and wide. The explosive emotions that accompanied it were a different story.

Zola was beautiful, but beyond that, she was sassy, confident, feisty, kind, compassionate and patient. With me, she'd still be her own woman and run her things like she was used to doing, but *all of her* would belong to me. I'd have no problem submitting to her, when need be, but she'd have no confusion as to who she belonged to... after God.

I often heard Jas and Rei, my cousin's wives, joke about my cousins' assertiveness. I snickered because I was 2.0. Intense. Formidable. Unyielding. Passionate. Those were some of the adjectives women had used to describe me. The only person that came close to handling it was Eno.

My eyes darted to the rearview mirror. *These ladies and their phones.* Uju was deeply engrossed in hers. Probably playing Roblox. I winced as "Shake It Off" by Taylor Swift came to an end on my speaker. The reason I knew the name of the song was because Uju commandeered the radio as soon as we got into the car. How she thought she could control my music and enjoy her game at the same time was a mystery to me.

"Ju, are you excited that you get to see your uncles?"

"Yes, daddy. I haven't seen them in a long time." Her big brown eyes met mine, her elation clear.

The familiar, overwhelming feeling of love filled my chest as our gazes met. A smile spread across my face.

Cheta had been on the road as the beginning of his final playoff season with the NBA was underway. He finally decided he wanted to retire, and I couldn't be happier for him. He'd also signed an initial, two-year contract for his ESPN show. In his words, he'd given all he had to the game, now it was time to give to his family. It was a beautiful thing to see how wide open he was over his wife.

Arinze had pulled back considerably on the number of movies he appeared in. His focus was more on the writing and consulting part of his business. That also required travel, so he too had been out of Atlanta for a couple of weeks. He and Jasmine had decided to get married in the courthouse then have their lavish wedding later. Before she could begin planning, they popped up pregnant. Since Jasmine refused to get married while pregnant, we were still waiting for their ceremony.

"But it's different now, daddy," Uju said, bringing me out of my thoughts.

We were on our way to the arcade and the whole family would be there. "What's different?"

"Us, everyone."

"How? It's always been 'Two Uncles, A Dad, and a Little Lady'." I teased, using the title we'd made up to mimic the popular movie.

She shrugged. "Uncle Nze and Auntie Jas will soon have their own baby, so won't have time anymore. Uncle C might be next." She sighed.

I wanted to say something. Pull over so I could hold her in my arms. Her painful tone wiped the feeling of joy I'd experienced a moment earlier. Despite my desperation to make her feel better, I needed to hear all she had to say. Whatever Zola told her the night before worked. This was the most open she'd been with me in months.

"I'm happy for my uncles, but before we used to hang out in the house together until I fell asleep, or one of them would come to school to eat lunch with me, but now... nothing. That makes me sad."

"But I'm here. Am I not enough?" Once the words left my mouth, I regretted them. Putting my newfound insecurity on my nine-year-old to assuage was low. But I really needed to know. Because even if I could get my cousins to adjust their schedules a little bit, Uju was still my responsibility. And the fact was, they did have wives who would always come first.

She met my eyes again and giggled. "You are daddy. But you travel a lot and I'm lonely sometimes. But you stay at home a lot more now so..."

"Is this why you're fighting and not doing well in school?"

She shook her head and looked down at her hands. "It's because one girl was teasing me. And Uncle C said I shouldn't let these suckers think I'm soft."

"He what?"

That sounded exactly like my cousin. It was no wonder when I told him she was fighting, he brushed it off. I needed to talk to him.

"How long has this been going on? I mean the teasing?"

"It started the day I went to school with my hair in a puff. You were on a trip and Eva took me to school, but she didn't do my hair well. When I got to school, one girl was pointing at me laughing. She said I looked like porcupine." Uju pouted her lips and folded her arms across her chest as though she was reliving the incident again.

"At first, I didn't answer her, Daddy, I promise. But then in another class, when the teacher was talking about the mother/daughter dance, those same girls started whispering to each other about how I don't have a mother, so I won't be able to go."

I lifted my eyes to the rearview mirror. "Mother/daughter dance? I've never heard you talk about that before."

"I'm in the fourth grade. It's only for fourth and fifth graders." She shrugged. "I don't want to go, anyway."

"Did they give you a flyer?" I glanced at her.

She nodded. Was she trying to spare my feelings by not showing it to me? I gripped the steering wheel so she wouldn't see my frustration. My daughter was being teased in school for not having a mother? I could see my mother and grandmother's faces giving me a hard stare. I could almost hear them saying, "All of this is happening because you won't take a wife."

I shook their voices out of my head. "When we get home, let me see the flyer, okay?"

She nodded again.

It was only March, and those things were normally in May. I'd see if Jas or Rei could free up their schedule for me…for her. As we continued our journey, Uju was like a tap whose water pressure caused it to burst. The incidents kept building until the day I went to eat lunch with her. A pang of guilt ripped through my chest because I should've pushed harder for an explanation. She withdrew and wouldn't say anything. That Zola got her to talk made me a little jealous, but grateful. I owed her.

A few minutes later, when she was done speaking, I reassured Uju about my schedule and reiterated that change was an important constant in life, but as a family, we'd adjust. Her smile returned and all was right in my world. I did a mental check of my schedule for Monday. It was packed with my class at the university, a few meetings at the studio, but before any of that, Uju's principal would see me. During the school day, they were entrusted with the safety and comfort of my child, and they had failed at both.

4

ZOLA

"I mean the nerve of him."

I crossed my legs and took a sip of the iced matcha latte in my hand. Waiting in the VIP area of Delta's Sky Club Lounge, I steadied the Bluetooth in my ear while my eyes roamed the room before landing on my watch. My mom had expected me to be on the first flight out of Atlanta, but that obviously didn't happen. She'd have to be okay with mid-morning.

I was still undecided about this blind date thing Tessa was setting up for me. Especially after last night. Men…Ugh.

I had the mind to cancel the trip to Luxe altogether, but when I listened to my mom's voicemail, threatening to come visit me if I didn't make it, I packed a bag. Her constantly rearranging things in the way she thought they should be, and me telling her that my things were the way I wanted them to be was a cycle I didn't have the capacity to go on with her right now.

I shook my head as Tessa's nauseating giggle winded down.

"It's not funny—"

"Yes, it is. You weren't even this rattled when you and Caleb were going through it. I mean you were upset, but not rattled."

The last thing I wanted to do was add Caleb Sterling to the

mental mess I was currently trying to untangle. The chaos that defined my week was trumped by Jidenna's unexpected arrival. The week had started off better than normal. All my teachers and students were on time. There weren't any unnecessary arguments. In addition to the regular class I taught, I had two performances and a competition to prepare for. Everything was running smoothly until Wednesday.

I got outside my condo and my two-month-old Audi Q7 wouldn't start. After tinkering with it for a while, I called for a tow. It took forever with the dealership, but I finally made it to work. Only to find out the vendor messed up the orders for the performance costumes. By the time I sorted that out and taught my classes, I realized the loaner car that was supposed to be sent over never came. I called the dealership and told them to forget the loaner since my car would be ready the next morning. It wasn't. Everything went downhill from there. Thursday wasn't any better and then Jidenna showed his ugly face the next day and I was done.

He's not ugly, but that's what I'm going with for now.

"Okay look, the way he went about it might have been wrong. But his intention was for you to be safe. Cut the man some slack."

"*E tu*, Tessa?"

Tessa laughed. "Is your flight delayed?"

As I was about to respond to her, the call for my flight echoed through the airport. I told her I'd see her soon before sending a text to my mother that I was heading to the gate. A few minutes later, as the plane began to taxi down the runway, my mind began to wander to last night.

In the three years that Uju had been enrolled in Leap & Twirl, I could confidently say she'd never been there a minute after closing. If I knew nothing else, I knew that Jidenna loved his daughter, and she was one of the most well-behaved little girls I knew. Their bond reminded me of the one I had with my dad. So when she had a whole tantrum because she'd been replaced as lead, I knew something had to be wrong.

Although I didn't know a lot about Jidenna except the little Jasmine and Reign had shared, I knew he was widowed. My mother not being there while I was growing up was an inconceivable thought for me, so I couldn't even begin to imagine how the little girl felt. After I had her sit out for the first thirty minutes of class, I went over to talk to her. Although I'd had interactions with her outside of the studio, I never expected her to open up to me. The tears and her pain spilled out from her mouth like a river bursting its banks.

A few hours later, despite the chill of the studio, I felt my office heat up and the hairs on the back of my neck stood. When my eyes locked with her father's, all the insults I'd rained over him, the stories I'd told myself about how unattractive he was, all withered away.

As he sauntered his lean but muscular frame toward me, I did a quick sweep of his features. Not that I needed to as they were committed to memory. But a refresher didn't hurt.

His low black hair was free of the cap I was used to him wearing, making his waves visible. The neatly trimmed connecting mustache and beard were a tell-tale sign of a recent visit to the barber's chair. His strong jawline, dark eyes, full nose, and lips were exactly how I'd remembered them.

My rage couldn't quench my raw need for him. It was undeniable. It was as if he had a gravitational pull on me that I couldn't resist. Pure visceral attraction. He was everything I wanted but told myself I didn't need. At least not anymore. When he sent his daughter out of the room and cornered me by my desk, I tried to maintain my composure. I was determined not to give him the satisfaction of knowing how much he affected me, but it was no use. My body betrayed me, and I could feel the heat rising in my cheeks.

When I tried to escape his grasp, my breath caught in my

throat as his grip tightened around my arm. I trembled, feeling a chill run through me. The masculine note of his scent made my head spin. His voice, needy but at the same time commanding, ignited a fire within me that had me saying a special prayer of thanks when Anna came into the room. By the time we got to my building, I was able to bring my body under subjection. All parts worked in tandem – except my heart – to keep me sane. My heart continued to pound. I thought it would pop out of my chest.

When I got to my apartment, I texted him as he asked. Something in his tone warned me that the hassle from doing otherwise wasn't worth it. Jidenna was the fire my mom warned me not to play with. Unlike when I was five years old, I intended to do just that.

~

"After all the fussing, neither of them was around to welcome me home," I muttered, stretching my body.

I sat up and slid my legs to the floor. That nap was so necessary. I arrived at Luxe Noir a few hours ago, and despite my asking my parents not to worry about me, I was greeted by Simon, my parents' driver when I stepped out of the airport. My dad was with his golf buddies while my mom had an emergency appointment in her office. Tessa was called in for an emergency at LGH.

Apart from the few staff my parents retained, the house was empty. I rolled my shoulders and strolled into the bathroom. A few moments later, I picked up my crossbody and headed for the stairs. The sun was out, and I was dying to visit The Cultural Commons. It was the vibrant community center located in Heritage Square. I'd spent many days there learning about the history of the town.

History had it that the illegal ship carrying about one hundred men, women and children docked on what is now known as Luxe Noir Island in the mid nineteenth century. The enslaved were a hodge podge of ethnic groups from present-day Nigeria, Guinea, Angola, Mali, Senegal, and Ghana. After the abolition of slavery and the Civil War, the men and women who settled in the island were joined by a few wealthy formerly enslaved people from the north.

The Cultural Commons was the hang out spot in the town. With high ceilings, natural light, and a mix of historic and modern architecture, it catered to performances, visual arts exhibits, community meetings, and socializing. I was particularly interested in the historic cultural displays. I needed inspiration for an African dance choreography for my students to perform in an upcoming competition.

As I descended the grand staircase of my childhood home, nostalgia hit. The plush carpet and ornate chandelier brought back memories of family occasions. The walls were decorated with paintings, family portraits, and mirrors that reminded me of stories my parents told of the house's history. Fresh flowers scented the air, as my mother was still obsessed with having floral arrangements in every common area. The Westbrooks were among Luxe Noir's first settlers and although the house had been gutted, restored, and modernized, it retained its character. Despite the passage of time and seasonal changes, the mansion still felt like home.

I strolled into the kitchen, opened the glass dome dessert plate on the island and took a freshly baked oatmeal cookie, then headed to the fridge for a bottle of water when Ms. Martha walked in. The older woman who had her own cottage on the estate had been our housekeeper and head of the house staff since I was about five years old. I called her the keeper of my teenage secrets. She always seemed to pop up when I was sneaking back into the house after curfew.

Her eyes went to the cookie in my hand, and she smiled. "Child, you'll ruin your appetite with that."

"Good afternoon, Ms. Martha. I'll be fine." I walked over and drew her into a hug. "I missed seeing you when I arrived."

"I was around here somewhere. Your mother said you should join them for dinner at the beach house by six."

After acknowledging the information, I chatted with her a little bit about what was going on in the town. It was small, so everyone knew everyone's business. My mom said that's why the community was close knit. I disagreed, but that's how Luxe Noir had survived for decades so who was I to change it? Leaving the kitchen soon after, I ran upstairs to get my carry-on, while texting Tessa about where I'd be. Since I was headed to the beach house later, I didn't want to have to come back here until tomorrow.

Stepping outside, I smiled at Simon as he rushed to open the car door for me.

"Thanks Si, but I'll walk." I took my carry-on to the car. "If you can meet me at the Square in a couple of hours, that'd be great."

After he acknowledged my request, I headed for the winding driveway to the gates, then the street. The salty ocean breeze tickled my nose while I soaked up the scarce warmth of the mid-March sun. My steps were accompanied by the rustling sound of fallen leaves as I walked down the stately, tree-lined street. Tessa, Zuri, and I spent many days roaming these same streets when we were younger. Before boys and heartbreak entered our lives. My older sister Zekia, had graduated, married, and moved to Italy by then.

Several minutes later, as I neared the Square, I heard music coming from the Commons – a familiar tune that stirred up a feeling of nostalgia within me. Taking a right turn, I entered the Commons, and was greeted by the comforting scents of coffee and baked goods. On the left side of the room, I could see a stage being prepared for an upcoming performance. I couldn't count the number of poetry readings, spoken word pieces and soulful tunes from local artists I'd listened to in this place. The highlight for me was to watch and be a part of dance rehearsals on that same stage. Steering my gaze toward the visual arts area, I made my way towards the historic pieces and photographs that were on display.

Grabbing my notepad, I fixed my attention on a black and white picture with a slight sepia tone. In the photograph stood a man and a woman from the 1900s. They were sharp for their day. The man had on a suit with a bow tie, while the woman had on a long skirt and blouse with a high collar. Both wore hats, and the man's hat tilted slightly to one side. Standing next to each other on a porch, they were smiling, although their expressions were somewhat serious. The description at the bottom read: The home of Odell and Eliza Jackson. "Bound by Chains. Freed by Love."

One of the three, freed Black men that came to the island from the north was Odell Jackson. He was the wealthiest of the trio and began buying up land. With the help of his friends and the families on the island, they began creating a self-sustaining community. In that time, his eye caught Eliza, one of the descendants of the original families from the Bambara tribe of present-day Guinea. Soon after, they got married. Their actual house was still on the island.

The house, the former schoolhouse and the grocery store were in good enough condition to be moved to a common area where tourists could visit at certain times of the year. Years ago, some residents formed an advocacy group to stand up against major development and to get Luxe Noir recognized in the National Register of Historic Places.

As I stared at the picture, my throat clogged. What they must have gone through. On their backs, Luxe Noir Island was born. Their descendants expanded into Luxe Noir Bay and over the decades, the residents of present-day Luxe Noir had been committed to preserving and maintaining the historical integrity of the community while also modernizing it to meet the contemporary standards of the town.

Over the next several minutes, my hands and brain worked at a fast pace, coming up with ideas. I jotted down the historical dance style and movements that would incorporate struggle, survival, triumph, and resilience. Ideas for costumes, color, props, and music all flowed into my notebook.

A few hours later, I leaned against the deck railing at my parents' beach house. The scent of salt water in the air and a cool breeze lifting my hair caused memories of the good, bad but not so ugly of years past to flood my mind. When I had arrived earlier, my parents lay in the hammock on the other side of the house enjoying a glass of wine. For as long as I could remember, my dad looked at my mom the same way. Like he'd stop breathing without her. That's what I wanted and thought I had found in Caleb, but oh boy, was I wrong. After we chatted for a bit, the chef announced that dinner would be ready in an hour, so we parted ways to freshen up. I was the first one down and as I gazed at the ocean, a familiar feeling washed over me.

I remembered the day I said, "I do." The beautiful ceremony was right in the backyard, and my parents spared no expense. At twenty- five, I'd gone exactly by the script. I'd gotten an education, secured a great job as a computer and information systems manager and found a man of equal status to marry. Caleb checked all those boxes, but unlike the horror stories of others who followed the Luxe Noir, high society script, I loved him. At least I thought I did.

"Darling, you'll get a chill."

Thankfully, my mother's voice cut short my trip into disaster-ville. I'd spent many nights analyzing where I went wrong, and I didn't want to do that tonight. Tonight, I wanted to enjoy my parents who I hadn't seen in a month.

"I'm fine, Mom, see I have a wrap. You look beautiful." The

weather was indeed a little chilly, but the light, short-sleeved sweater I had on was perfect for the evening. Before she could provide a rebuttal, my dad walked in.

Richard Westbrook was a tall, distinguished sixty-nine-year-old. His deep brown skin, salt and pepper hair, and resonant voice were features I didn't appreciate about my father when I was younger. Especially when he'd visit my high school. The girls would giggle and stare at him puppy eyed. I still cringed thinking about them commenting on him being their crush. With age and maturity, I accepted the fact that my dad and my four brothers who looked like him were some fine, debonaire Black men. It was so hard to make friends because all the girls, except Tessa, wanted one of the Westbrook boys.

"Looking good, Daddy. Let me find out that you out here in these streets looking all good..." I allowed the insinuation that he was looking good for other ladies to linger. It was a joke that he caught on to and apparently so did my mother.

My dad smiled then kissed my mom on her cheek while pulling out her chair. "Thank you, princess."

My dad walked over and did the same for me. I felt the steam from my mom's eyes, so I turned to face her. "Did I say anything wrong, Mother?" I struggled to stifle my laughter.

"Keep playing with me, young lady."

I chuckled. My mother, the always composed, regal and graceful woman I'd grown up knowing, now swore she was "down" too. After she retired from actively practicing family law, my mother founded the Westbrook Legal Empowerment Fund. The fund focused on empowering marginalized people through legal aid and advocacy. Because of her work, and her aim to relate to the younger generation, her staff was diversified in class and age. This apparently made her think she knew the appropriate way to use most slang. The first day I heard her say, "It's giving..." I almost fainted.

Minutes later, dinner was served, we said grace and began to eat. Although my dad answered questions he was asked and contributed to the conversation, I could sense he was distracted. My mother noticed it sometimes too, and he kissed the back of her hand to deflect her questions. My heart raced at the possibility that something was wrong with his health.

Sitting here with my parents, I realized how deep my love for them went. They had provided such an amazing childhood for me and my siblings. And they were still loving and supportive of us in whatever way we needed. They were golden. The thought that something might be wrong with my dad plunged me into a spiral of fear. I hated to think of a day when he and my mom wouldn't be there for me.

"Dear, don't forget, next week Zuri and I are going to New York to interview some of her designer choices." My mother's voice interrupted my moment of worry. "We would need the jet and your card, of course." She then turned to me. "You should come with us."

I frowned. That would be a negative. Only my baby sister would want well known, luxury, Black designers to vie for her money. My dad's money, but same thing. Whoever she picked would design the whole wedding party. I loved it for her, but I couldn't sit through that.

My dad nodded, lifting a shrimp to his mouth. "When is she coming home? I haven't seen my baby girl in–"

"She'll be here next week."

"At least one of them came to see me." My dad reached across the table and squeezed my hand. "I thought for a minute you'd be bringing someone to see me," he said.

My brows came together, and I pushed my empty plate forward. "Who?"

"That young man we saw you plastered all over the internet with," my mom supplied.

"Jidenna?" I cocked my head to the side. "And we were not plastered all over the internet. It was one event for charity."

"And the NBA championship parade," my mother said.

I gave her a fake smile.

My dad raised his brow. "So?"

"Daaaddy…"

"Stop whining. Your father wants to know if there is anything we should know," my mother said, wiping the corners of her mouth.

I laughed. This woman never ceased to amaze me, and the funniest part was her husband went along with her schemes. "Do yooouuu want to know, Daddy?"

My dad shifted uncomfortably in his chair. To save him from my mother's mouth later, I continued. "There is absolutely nothing between Jidenna and I."

My mother shrugged. "Just as well."

I rolled my eyes. One of the perils of being from a wealthy family was that your parents viewed anyone interested in you under the microscope of "gold digger." My heart broke for my older sister when she brought Antonio home. Not only was he a blue-collar guy, but he also wasn't Black.

"Mom, that man needs nothing from me. He has his own—"

"Hush, child. I know who he is. Do you think my daughter would be photographed with someone in various publications, and I not find out who he is?" She straightened her shoulders and tucked her curly hair behind her ears. "I know he is a Kalu. I know of his family's status. I know his status and that of his famous cousins. What I meant was he's a widowed, single father from a different culture. Those relationships can be hard and not something I'd want for you. I want your next marriage to be your last marriage."

"Naomi," my dad warned. He only used my mother's name when it was time to rein her in.

His timing was devastatingly spot on because that last part hurt. My parents had been married for over forty years without scandal. They were the embodiment of Black love, and here I was, the one who single-handedly tainted the Westbrook name with the perceived blemish of divorce.

During my two-year marriage, I had lived in Houston, but after the divorce, I quit my job and returned home. While they never uttered it aloud, I felt their disappointment seep through every conversation, and every look in my direction. Not only from them, but the whole town. The months I stayed to grieve the loss of my dreams and hope for the future were pure hell. When I saw the Leap & Twirl post on LinkedIn, I contacted Mrs. Donovan. The desire to return to a passion that had been snuffed out by family pressure was reignited, so without a second thought, I moved to Atlanta for a fresh start. It'd been years, but occasionally, I'd still be reminded that I had made an irreversible mistake.

"Believe it or not, I want the best for you," my mother said. Her tone was softer while she placed her hand over mine and squeezed.

That was the closest I'd ever get to an apology, so I nodded. My dad, like the protector he'd always been, quickly navigated us to other topics. Soon our dinner plates were replaced with cheesecake and black tea. My mother restated her demand for me to attend and judge the talent part of the Divine Soirée. Then she talked about her end-of-year gala with the usual expectation that all her children be there.

Despite how worrisome she could be, I felt grateful for this moment. The chance to sit down with both my parents in a house that had always been surrounded by love, comfort, and support. As my parents continued to chat, my thoughts went to Jidenna. After the evening we spent together, I remembered lying across my bed in the early hours of the morning, envisioning our nuptials. My divorce didn't deter me from love, but after he went ghost on me, I forced myself to accept the possibility that I might never get to experience what my parents had.

The next morning, loud noises woke me from sleep. Feeling

for my phone, I found it under the pillow and lifted it to my face. Peeling my eyes open, I realized it was a little after six a.m. On Sundays, my parents normally didn't get up until eight, then we'd all drive to town to attend church.

Last night after dinner, I headed into town to meet with Tessa at a local lounge. Returning just after midnight, I showered and was out for the count a few seconds later.

"I cannot believe you," my mother yelled.

The next sound I heard was a deafening crash. My eyes flew open in shock and my breathing quickened as I leapt out of bed. Quickly putting on my robe, I raced out of the room. My feet hit the cold tile, reminding me I didn't have on my slippers. Not bothering to go back, I raced down the stairs. As I stumbled into the kitchen, I heard a defeated voice that chilled me to the core.

"MiMi, I didn't mean to—"

My mind raced with all sorts of horrific possibilities as I saw my parents standing on opposite sides of the kitchen island. Shards of broken plates littered the floor. Did my dad cheat on my mom? Heavy tension hung in the air as I looked between them, seeing anger and remorse collide in my dad's eyes, while my mother's were filled with rage. I couldn't believe these were the same people wrapped in each other's arms hours earlier.

"What's going on? What's wrong?" My voice quivered as fear surged through me, dreading what their answer might be.

Their eyes remained locked on each other, but my mother spoke. "Go ahead, Richard. Explain to your daughter how you could go years deceiving your family."

"Naomi, if you'll just listen to me—"

"Listen to what? How we'll be the laughingstock of Luxe Noir? How we—"

I pulled the silk scarf off my head because at this point, they were driving me crazy. "Can someone please tell me what's going on? Please."

My dad's face fell as he slowly exhaled, his shoulders seeming to drop an inch lower. His gaze moved from the tiled floor up to mine, and I saw something there I'd never seen before—shame, like a heavy blanket draped over him. My heart tugged in my chest, but I held my tongue.

"I made some bad investments," he started, his voice cracking slightly, "and despite all my efforts, the bank has given me one month to pay them off, or they'll seize our property."

The words hung in the air and echoed around us. A strange stillness filled the kitchen as I processed the information. Before I could even respond, my mother spoke with icy fury.

"What your father is trying to say," she snapped, "is that we're broke, and in about thirty days, we'll be homeless." With those words, she spun on her heel and strode out of the room.

5

JIDENNA

"That principal is so lucky you went up there and not me," Cheta said, his eyes fixed on the 72-inch TV mounted on the wall in my gaming room.

Among all the rooms in my home, this dimly lit space was my favorite. It even beat out my mini studio most days and was off limits to everyone else except my cousins. The room was decorated with a few framed posters of classic video games and an impressive collection of gaming consoles and controllers, arranged neatly on a shelf. We were currently lounging on the massive, leather sofa engaged in a heated game of FIFA 22.

Arinze looked over at him. "You're a whole husband and still your first go-to is violence."

Cheta took his eyes of the screen and turned to Arinze. "First of all, a nice read is not violence and two, is marriage supposed to change who I am at the core?"

"No, it's not, but it's supposed to—"

"*Abeg* leave that thing." Cheta waved him off then faced me. "Nna, for real though, is everything squared away with JuJu and the school?"

"She's been behaving better, and I haven't gotten any calls

from the school. But she still walks around here some days like she has the weight of the world on her shoulders."

Arinze set down his controller to answer his buzzing phone. "I'm sure it's a phase." His smile widened as he answered the Facetime call.

"*Obi m*, wassup baby?" he asked.

"I'm fine, babe, just checking in. I know how you get," Jasmine said.

"As long as you know. You and my son can't be galivanting Atlanta without checking in."

"I know it's pointless reminding you that we are nowhere close to knowing the sex of this baby."

Arinze smirked. "Haven't you heard the expectation of the righteous shall not be cut short?"

"Okay, y'all need to take that somewhere. Nze, are you still playing or are you going to be caking all day?" Cheta asked.

I laughed. Cheta made it his mission to tease Jasmine every chance he got. Pausing the game, I went to the bar in the corner and opened the mini fridge.

"C, how many times do I have to tell you green doesn't look good on you," Jasmine fired back.

"Jazzy Jas, ain't nobody hating on you, but you messing up our game," he said. Taking the phone from Arinze, he continued. "In fact, where's my wife? Tell her to call me. I'm in the mood to cake to."

"Che bear, you miss me? I'll call you in a minute. My nails are wet," Reign yelled in the background.

"What I tell you about calling me that in public?" Cheta asked in feigned annoyance.

"Oh, so you answer to corny names in private," I teased. "Good to know."

Cheta cut his eyes at me, then Arinze as we laughed at him. He was always trying to boss up on somebody.

"Y'all leave my baby alone," Reign fussed.

I walked up to the phone with three bottles of Malt in my hand. "Ain't nobody bothering your big baby. But where my baby at?"

"She's fine. They're finishing up her braids right about now," Reign said.

As a family, we attended first service at our church, then gathered in my home for Sunday brunch. Soon after, while my cousins hung back, the ladies took Uju out for a day of pampering. Hair, nails, and facials. The full works.

"Appreciate y'all for hooking my princess up."

"How did my conversation turn into a family chat?" Arinze stood, snatched his phone and walked out of the room with his drink in his hand.

"I guess that's that." Cheta headed to the restroom.

I tidied up a little and soon after, they both walked back into the room. We lounged around and discussed a little about the family. Although none of us played an active role in Kalu International Inc., we all sat on the board and gave input on some business decisions. Our Lagos Tune Up location was finally ready for launch. Tune Up was the full-service, male grooming salon my cousins and I owned in Nigeria. The Enugu location had been up and running for a few years now. So we decided to expand.

"I'm glad my niece is better." Arinze took a sip of his drink. "If things continue this way, you can avoid the woman aunty and *nne anyi ukwu* will have lined up for you in Naija."

The randomness of his comment put a frown on my face. It'd been weeks since my mother and our grandma left. When I told my cousins about their threat, we all laughed about it, but really didn't address it again.

Cheta laughed. "Who knows, they might've held their auditions in secret this time since cuz spoiled their runs the last time."

Arinze narrowed his eyes at Cheta who was now bent over on the sofa laughing. I followed suit because that was the funniest thing ever. About three years ago, after one of Uju's dance recitals, while Zola was telling me of Uju's potential in dance, I heard a loud cackle from Cheta. Walking over to where he and Arinze stood, I was handed Arinze's phone. On it was a video that Ifunanya, Arinze's younger sister sent of our grandmother openly auditioning a woman for Arinze to marry. That quickly led him to Rent A Bae, a dating agency, and subsequently the love of his life, Jasmine.

"I'm glad she's better because I want her to be happy, not because I fear an arranged marriage. Unlike both of you, I'm not afraid of entering such a marriage for her sake if I have to," I said.

They both looked at me with bugged eyes.

I shrugged. I wasn't. I went on to explain my thoughts to my cousins who both looked at me with their scowls deepening with every point I gave. The current dating scene was trash, and I wasn't ready for the stress. In an arranged marriage, both parties went into the union with eyes wide open. Both families were involved, eliminating, or minimizing the stress of family bickering. Both parties also entered the arrangement with a common goal of commitment and stability without the huge sacrifices often made when one's heart was involved. Everyone was on the same page with no outrageous expectations. In a nutshell, it didn't come with the complication of love.

After a few moments of silence, rubbing his earlobe, Arinze spoke first. "So, you're willing to marry a stranger because you don't want to be stressed?"

"I mean—"

"Nze, you're going too far talking about stress," Cheta said, looking me dead in the eye. "So, let me understand this right. You'd put my niece through the agony of having a stepmother she has no rapport with simply because you don't want family bickering?" He pointed his index finger to his temple before asking. "*O we ife ne me gi nisi?* Are you okay?"

I laughed at him and Arinze trying to son me because my

views differed from theirs. I was used to it. Me being the youngest, they'd done this all my life.

"Just because you don't get along with your in-laws doesn't mean I want that life," I teased. It was no secret that Cheta and Reign's parents weren't fond of each other. The first day he met them, they walked him out of their house.

Cheta thumbed his nose. "My wife's folks are good with me as long as they talk to her like they have some sense. I don't care who they are. If they disrespect her, I'm getting on them every single time. And I'll sleep good at night."

"You know this guy talks reckless, so I wonder why you brought that up," Arinze said.

"Anyway, what I said was, I'm not afraid of an arranged marriage. Uju's opinion will always factor in. Her *reasonable* opinion. In fact, at this point, the reason I would get married would be for her sake. For her to have a good mother".

"*Nwoke m puo ebe a.* Just say you're afraid of love," Arinze said. "That I get."

Cheta nodded in agreement. "I know, right? That's why he ran away from Teach," Cheta added, referring to Zola by the nickname he'd given her.

"What if I am? I've been there! Love is pain." I hit my fist on my chest.

"So, what's your plan here? To stay single forever? My niece needs a mother. Granted you protect her from the women you rotate, but she needs a stable mother figure," Arinze said.

"Jokes aside, it's not only about you and protecting yourself. It's about JuJu," Cheta said.

"Look at this guy. Been married for two minutes and now wants to lecture me," I scoffed.

"I don't care about you or your tantrum, really. All I care about is my niece," Cheta fired back.

When we were younger, Cheta and I, who are closer in age, would get to fighting on the slightest provocation. His volume was higher, but I knew how to scrap, just like he did. I'm not gonna pretend like I whooped his behind, but I never went down without leaving a mark on him. Now, we argued, then gave each other room to breathe. I knew my cousins had my best interest at heart, but I didn't need the lecture from them. Before they were men enough to put rings on their wives' fingers, I did that with Eno because I recognized my love for her and went after what I wanted.

"Y'all calm it down," Arinze chimed in like he always did.

My eyes darted to Cheta scrolling through his phone. A sign of his annoyance. I chuckled.

"You loved Eno… I can't go too many hours without hearing from my wife. A text, a call, something, so I can't fathom how devastating her death was for you. In all that, you had a newborn, so you had to shove your feelings aside for her sake. Then when Uju got a little older, you drowned yourself in work, but Nna, it's been almost ten years," Arinze pleaded.

"You know we got you. And you're a great father, but JuJu needs a mother. We're not saying go out and marry someone grandma picks for you for the sake of getting Juju a mother. We're saying be open to the possibility of a real relationship," Cheta said. He looked at me with only brotherly love in his eyes, all the heat from the argument gone. Then he smirked. "If after all is said and done, you don't find someone that can potentially be a suitable wife, I'll personally pay for nationwide auditions for you."

Arinze laughed and I shook my head. He could never be serious.

Cheta stared at something on his phone before lifting his eyes to me. "Start with Teach. Her peoples got money, so gold digger eliminated."

"Something is wrong with you," Arinze said.

Cheta shrugged.

Ready to be done with this conversation, I nodded. "I hear

y'all. Now can we get back to the game before the women get back?"

"Fire it up." Arinze scooted to the edge of the sofa while Cheta set it up.

Zola had been heavy on my mind since we reconnected two days ago. A stranger could see there was no chemistry lost between us. The issue was getting her to soften up a little so I could explain my actions and hopefully get her to forgive me. Then I could work on regaining her trust. Uju adored Zola and watching them interact with such a level of comfort filled my mind with the possibilities. Pulling out my phone, I went to her contact. All messages I had sent her since Friday had gone unanswered. I smiled because she wouldn't let me half step. I loved that. I typed out a text.

> You still mad at me?

I was pleasantly surprised when seconds later, I saw the three text bubbles appear.

Zola: Leave me alone.

> I can't do that.

Zola: You did it for months, try harder.

I smiled. A wave of relief washed over me. She was still angry. As long as she wasn't indifferent, anger, I could handle.

Several hours later, I lifted my eyes from the sketch book on my drafting table when I heard the door to my home studio open.

"Daddy, I have finished my homework. It's time."

Setting my pencil down, I watched Uju skip towards me. I

was designing a limited-edition collaborative collection of accessories for Zeidu Fashions. We'd finally closed the deal that we began negotiations on several months ago. The pieces would be launched with their next year spring line. We'd agreed on a mixture of metal scraps and discarded fabric that would highlight my artistic vision and their commitment to sustainability.

I helped Uju up on the stool so she could get a proper look. She'd been using that stool to keep me company while I sketched since she was old enough to hold her head up.

"Oh Daddy, it's pretty. It looks like an earring," she said.

"That's because it is an earring." I kissed her temple.

"But I thought you made all those other ugly pieces."

I gasped in feigned hurt. "Ju, you think daddy's art is ugly?"

She giggled. "Okay, maybe not like super-duper ugly. But I mean you really, really have to look closely to see how beautiful it is."

I laughed. "That's because its abstract and I use materials most people recycle or throw away."

She leaned closer to the drawings. "Okay." She pointed at each design. "But I like these earrings, and this bangle...oooh I like this pendant, Daddy. Are they for me?"

"Kids that say their daddy's art is ugly don't get these accessories." I winked.

"Ooof, that's rough. Good thing I'm not one of those kids."

Laughing, I helped her down from the stool and closed my sketch book. "What is it time for?"

She let out a labored breath. "You forgot? Come on, Daddy, you promised to practice the *tendu* with me." She grabbed my hand, pulling me out of the room. "I want to show Ms. Zola that I can do all the steps without mistakes."

"You like Ms. Zola?"

"Yes! She's the best." Uju halted abruptly, almost making me knock her over. "Do you like her, Daddy?"

"What makes you ask that?"

She shrugged and continued walking. "That day you came late, you were looking at her the way those gross boys look at the girls in the program Ms. Eva watches." She took a breather, then continued, "They always look like that before they kiss." She shook her head then finished with, "Eww."

I was stunned. I didn't know what part of her narrative to focus on. One thing I did know was I had to have a conversation with Eva about what she allowed Uju to watch. At least she still thought boys were gross. That was a good thing. We entered her playroom and walked over to the side of the room that served as her mini studio. I had the area remodeled, complete with vinyl flooring, a wall of mirrors and the horizontal handrail used for support.

"You didn't answer my question, Daddy."

"What question is that?"

"Do you like Ms. Zola?"

"I guess so. Now, first position, extend your right foot forward, toes pointed, heel on the ground, then slide back," I called out the routine for her.

I had popped into her room one day and she was on her bed, sad. After I inquired, she explained how she was struggling with the *plie* and *tendu*. Immediately, I got online to study the routines. I knew that if I could learn the steps myself, then I could help her through them as well. I laughed at myself as I practiced the routines in my bedroom, but I was down for anything that made my daughter's life easier.

Now, watching her repeat the *tendu* eight more times and getting better with each try put a satisfied grin on my face. Her smile was priceless, and there was nothing I wouldn't do to keep it in place. Even if it meant getting back into the dating arena so she could have the mother I knew she desperately wanted.

6

―――――――

ZOLA

The relief was slow, but I was so thankful it was finally coming along. I readjusted the heating pads at my lower back and abdomen. I groaned and clenched my teeth as another round of pain hit. The intensity felt like someone was stabbing me with a hot knife repeatedly. I gripped the sheets and waited out the intensity of the cramps coming in waves.

Endometriosis.

I'd been diagnosed since my late teens. My periods were short, lasting three or four days. The short span, however, wasn't one I dared without strong medication. Over the years, I had undergone two surgeries and tried many medications. I even started hormonal therapy. Between doctors, specialists and medications, I had managed to live with minimal pain from my symptoms. This month however, I wasn't so lucky. I might have been totally wrong, but I knew my stress level had something to do with it.

I took a deep breath, struggling to control my breathing. My eyes darted to my phone on the nightstand of my darkened bedroom. Wednesday, noon, and I was still in bed. I had things to do, but I knew I wouldn't be going anywhere today.

Instead of the chill weekend I had expected, I was caught in the middle of my parents' fighting. It had gotten so bad that I took my mom with me to town while I asked my dad to stay at the beach house until I calmed her down. I could see the hurt, disappointment, and betrayal in her eyes. To know that the person you trusted with your future had fumbled it and kept it a secret for two whole years…

However, in my dad's defense, it was the first time, and he was trying to fix the problem before she found out about it because he knew this would be her reaction. My mother could easily get the money from her dad, my grandad, to fix the problem, but my dad would lose his respect and never hear the end of it. My father forbade her from asking her family, and that angered her the more. These were stressors I didn't need.

I heard my front door chime, and soon after, the alarm was disabled. "Zee, it's me," Tessa called out.

Needing to get away, I left Luxe without telling Tessa. She had already called to let me have it the day before. Earlier, she called because she needed to ask me something, but heard the wails from my excruciating pain instead. So, as we always were for each other, she was here. She couldn't stay the night, but according to her, she needed to lay eyes on me. I didn't have the energy to yell out to her, so I remained silent. She'd find me eventually.

"Oh, my poor baby," she said.

I peeled open my eyes to see her silhouette in the room. She knew not to turn on the lights or open the shades. Instead, she walked over to my nightstand and looked at my medications.

"Have you taken them?"

I nodded.

"Have you eaten anything?"

"I can't," I whispered.

"I'll make you some soup. You can't pump these meds into

your body without eating anything." She walked towards my bedroom door. "I'll be right back."

A few hours later, I moved to the living room with my heating pads in tow. The pain was better, and I prayed it stayed that way. Tessa was a godsend. Placing the bowl of chicken soup on the coffee table, I lifted the cup of lemon, ginger, turmeric tea to my lips and took a soothing sip. The warmth of the tea spread down my throat, soothing the walls of my stomach. The last twenty-four hours had been tough.

As I sat back on the couch, I noticed a shadow moving in my peripheral. Leaning my head to the side, I caught Tessa staring at me.

"Wassup?" I asked.

She narrowed her eyes at me and walked closer to the couch. She had been on a call about a conference she would be attending in New York in a few days. Sitting cross-legged opposite me, she kept her gaze on me, then shook her head before rubbing her temple.

"What? You're freaking me out, giving me those weird looks."

"How are you feeling?" she asked.

"Better... but you know the usual." I didn't have it in me to elaborate or describe my pain. Tessa was a part of my journey; she knew what I was going through.

"Have you given any more thought to what your doctor said?"

I cradled my head, wishing the floodgate of my tear ducts to remain shut. I remembered the message preached this past Sunday. No matter how mad my mother got, she was going to attend church come Sunday morning. After the whole fiasco at the beach house, I just wanted to sit with my thoughts, trying to process all my dad shared. But when she knocked on my bedroom door asking me to go with her, I did. Especially since I had pleaded with my dad to stay away from the house.

I wasn't a heathen, but since becoming an adult, although I believed there was benefit in the gathering of the flock, I no longer believed that if I didn't go to an actual building, I was the devil's spawn.

I was glad I went. The pastor talked about how humans walk around with the illusion of control, planning out our lives without consulting the One who gave us life. When in reality, we didn't have control over anything.

I dropped my gaze to the floor, feeling the weight of what I was about to say. "I know that my body has the potential to heal if I have a child. That was supposed to be part of my happily ever after. But that didn't work out, now did it?" I sighed heavily and ran a hand through my hair. "My family already thinks I'm a black sheep. Having a child out of wedlock would kill my mother." I shook my head slowly, steeling myself against the idea. "I can't do it, Tess."

"I feel you. Your wails break my heart every time. It—"

"Besides, I don't want a baby by myself." I chuckled. "I'm too spoiled for that."

"That you are."

"Don't even go there. You're the same way."

"No, I'm not." She laughed. "I fell into money when I was ten, you were born with money."

I admired Tessa's stepdad so much. He wasn't one of those men that thought a woman who had a child was tainted. He saw Tessa's mother and went after her. Their story was beautiful.

"Okay, my sis. I'll intensify my prayers for you to find Prince Charming soon. I thought the Nigerian Prince would be the one, but oh well."

I cackled, shaking my head because she was referring to Jidenna. "You do know that is hella stereotypical." I hadn't told her of the night he came to the studio. There was no need since I didn't plan on entertaining him again or hearing his explanation.

She waved me off and rolled her eyes. "I know, my bad. I'm mad at him ghosting you like that." A beat passed between us before she spoke again. "Okay, so are you ready to tell me what made you run from Luxe?"

I took a deep breath. Yesterday, I called all my brothers to try and feel them out, but none of them seemed to know what was going on. I wasn't surprised. If my mom hadn't overheard my dad in the bathroom asking his financial advisor to look for buyers for the family yacht, she wouldn't have known. Since my siblings didn't know, I contemplated telling Tessa, but I needed to get this off my chest. Telling my sisters would be upsetting, especially Zuri. She'd fly into a frenzy since my dad was responsible for her upcoming wedding.

"My dad…I mean, my family is in big financial trouble."

"What? How? How does a millionaire many times over have financial troubles?"

I scratched my head. "I wondered the same thing when I woke up to my parents arguing at dawn. Tess, I've never seen my mother so upset. And I felt so bad for my dad because he was trying to talk to her. I don't think it's so much the money as it is the secrets."

Tessa's brows furrowed. "I'm still confused."

"So, remember the time when the Feds dropped the interest rate? Well, that laxity with the interest rates caused his financial advisors to make some bad investments. Then he made investments in tech and crypto that weren't smart." I shook my head. "I mean they didn't live up to their hype and the regulators were breathing down their necks. Then the pandemic happened. He tried to keep things afloat by taking out additional loans on the houses…both of them."

My dad was a smart man. Westbrook Equity Group was what it was today because of his business acumen. My grandfather started the company in the 1930s as Westbrook Motors, with the manufacture of engines. My dad, an investment banker, pivoted with the times and decided to own equity in other firms and startups. I guess greed was real because he was so busy flying off the wave of getting richer that he didn't even stop to do his due dili-gence. I loved my dad, and I would do anything to help him out, but I didn't get my trust fund for another four years. Not like he would take it from me anyway.

"Girl, it's a mess. Now he needs ten million in liquid cash to keep from losing the houses—"

"But I don't get it. Didn't they give him time? How can the bank come and repo the house?"

"That's the thing. This has been going on for almost two years. If he had said something earlier, maybe my mom would have worked with him. I know she still will, 'cause Naomi loves her some Richard. She's just giving him a hard time now."

"Wow. I don't even know what to say." She paused. "Remember in that economics class we took in LNU?"

I nodded. Luxe Noir University was the historically Black college Tessa and I attended.

"I'll never forget when the professor said something along the lines of, when the tides go out, then you find out who has been swimming naked. I mean, no shade…but man."

That was a paraphrase from Warren Buffet. I couldn't even be mad because she was right. For almost two years, none of us had a clue as to what was going on. Tessa was about to say something else when my phone started ringing. Glancing at the caller ID, I saw it was my mother. Sighing, I picked up the phone and showed the screen to Tessa who chuckled. "I love my mother, but in the past forty-eight hours, she has called me to death complaining about my dad. I'm not even sure I ever wanna get married again."

Tessa stood, picked up my bowl and headed to the kitchen. "Don't do Aunty MiMi. Her feelings are hurt."

"Good afternoon, Mom," I greeted.

"Hello darling, how are you?"

I could sense the sadness in her voice. She was already dealing with a lot. There was no need to offload my present anguish on her. Besides there wasn't anything she could do for me.

"I'm okay, mom. How are you feeling?"

I listened to my mother describe her normal day like she wasn't crumbling on the inside. I'm sure if I were to Facetime her, she would be dressed to the nines and not a single strand of her thick, black hair would be out of place. Tessa came back into the room and gestured to her wrist. I knew she had to head to the airstrip where her father's jet was waiting. I raised my index finger, asking for an extra minute.

"Did you hear me, darling?" my mother asked.

"Sorry Mom, what did you say?"

"I asked if you wouldn't mind coming home as soon as possible. Your father will send the jet your way. It's important."

I stood. "Is everything okay?"

"It will be."

I wanted to probe further, but I got the sense that she wouldn't give up any details. "And it can't wait until the weekend?"

"It would be better if you came as soon as possible." Impatience seeped through her voice.

I did a quick mental check of my schedule. I didn't have anything really pressing until Friday, but that didn't mean I didn't have things to do. The bigger issue was that nothing in me wanted to be in the middle of my parents right now.

"Mom, I must be back by Friday morning." I watched as Tessa slung her bag over her shoulder.

"And you will be. The pilot will give you a call once he lands."

"Never mind, Tessa is here. I'll fly back with her."

My mother asked to speak to Tessa. I handed over the phone and made my way to my room. I had no idea what my parents wanted. The only silver lining was that whatever it was, they were working together to get it.

~

Unbelievable.

I couldn't believe what my parents were telling me. My eyebrows dipped and my eyes darted between my dad, seated at his mahogany desk, and my mom standing next to him. I was growing increasingly dissatisfied with the conversation. Surely this wasn't why they called me here.

I stood up, walked over to the wall, and leaned against it while making sure not to disturb the painting as I did so. Folding my arms across my chest, I waited a few beats then turned back to them.

"Zola, did you hear me?" my dad asked.

His tone was low, the desperation evident, but my gaze remained on the large gold "W" emblazoned on the desk.

"Darling, your father needs this. The family needs—"

"Mom, I know that, but what you're asking me to do is—"

"Baby girl, all I'm asking, is for you to use your relationship with the man to ask if he will reconsider..."

"But dad, that's just it. I don't have a relationship with him. Despite the stories the blogs and internet continue to speculate on, Jidenna and I are not anything." I flailed my arms. "I teach his daughter dance and that's it," I explained for like the third time since I'd gotten here.

The driver was waiting at the airport to pick me up and take me home, but instead, he took me to the downtown building that housed Westbrook Equity Group. I had an inkling something was up when I stepped through the large, oak wood door of my dad's office on the top floor. When my mom appeared by his side, pushing imaginary lint off his gray suit jacket, it confirmed my suspicions. But nothing prepared me for what they wanted me to do.

"Zola, it can't be that bad. We saw pictures of the two of you

at the gala and again when his cousin won the basketball championship. You didn't look like enemies," my mother said.

"I'm not saying we are." I turned to my father. "Daddy, explain
this to me again. Art? How?"

My dad stood and moved in front of his desk. Despite his
worry, his gait was as confident and regal as it always was. He
leaned on it and stretched his hand out for my mother who
promptly took it. They were so nauseatingly Black love-ish.
Their united front was something I always admired, but right
now, I wished one of them could see through my eyes that this
was crazy.

"I was at the golf course and Fred started talking about this
big global exhibit taking place in New York. It's supposed to be a
culmination of art pieces from around the world that showcase
precolonial historic artifacts…"

I zoned out listening to my dad explain what he had told me
earlier. Apparently, the sponsors of the exhibit wanted these
ancient masks that belonged to some tribe of Nigeria. The
problem now was that the masks had recently been acquired by
one person who had a principle of not leasing historic artifacts to
museums outside the African shores. That person happened to be
the current thorn in my side—Jidenna Kalu.

Now I was supposed to ask him if he could bend his rule
because of my relationship with him. A relationship that was
nonexistent. I had been ignoring his texts and while I knew he
could pop up on me at any time, I was glad he hadn't. I heard his
apology, but I was too angry to care. I was going to have to see
him on Friday since his daughter's class had their quarterly Twirl
with Dad, but now instead of ignoring him, I was going to have
to play nice because my dad *needed* this.

"Darling, your father and I sat down with the financial advisors. Everything has been restructured properly." She looked up
at my father. Nothing in her starry-eyed gaze suggested she
wanted to kill him a few days ago. "In less than six months and

with a few adjustments, everything will go back to normal. However, the bank wouldn't extend any additional credit at this time. If—"

"As you know, ten million dollars in liquid cash will get both houses back in good standing." My dad cleared his throat. "That collection is valued at twenty-five million dollars with the forty percent brokerage commission..."

"And you want to be the broker?" I asked, not really needing an answer. "We have like three weeks before the bank comes knocking. Are you sure you'll get the money on time? I know you haven't told my brothers, but if you did, they could help."

My parents were very proud of what they had accomplished over the years. I knew he wouldn't ask his friends for help, and that's why he was secretly trying to sell off his assets. My mother would never agree to that for fear of the town talk. But my brothers could do something.

My dad shook his head. "Fred assured me that if I can get it, all funds would be handled swiftly. The sponsors have been trying to get Kalu to agree for months, so they are ready." He rose to his full height. "The fact that *you* are even involved breaks my heart. I don't want to alarm anyone else. I'm—"

"What makes you think Jidenna will make an exception for me?" I let out a deep sigh.

"Darling, you are a Westbrook—more importantly, you are my daughter. I think you know how to use your appeal and powers of persuasion to *convince* him," my mother said.

In other words, seduce him.

My father gave her a harsh look, but kept silent. So, it seemed it was up to me to be the Esther of the Bible to save the Westbrook family.

Was I willing to sell my soul to save the family homes?

7

JIDENNA

Monday morning, I sat at the kitchen table, sipping my morning coffee. I scrolled through my emails as I waited for Uju so I could take her to school. Moments later, I heard the soft patter of footsteps approaching. Looking up, I saw her making her way towards me. There was a worried expression etched across her face. My heart sank. This merry-go-round we were on was taking a toll on our relationship. One week she was my lively princess, the next she was closed off and moody. There hadn't been any fighting incidents, but her temperament often got the best of her. Her apprehension on approach already told me that I wasn't going to like what she had to say.

"Good morning, Daddy."

"Good morning, princess," I greeted her, trying to mask my concern. "What's the matter?"

Uju hesitated for a moment before placing a folded piece of paper on the table, avoiding eye contact. My gaze shifted to the document, recognizing it as the dreaded school conduct paper that required my signature.

I took a deep breath, steeling myself as I opened it. Reading the document, I lifted my eyes.

"Obianuju Kalu, yelling in class? What is wrong with you? Do you want to go to Enugu to live with your grandma? Because you're getting really close, young lady." I rarely used her full name so when I did, she knew I meant business and now I did.

Tears filled her eyes. I wanted to comfort her, but I couldn't keep coddling her.

"Explain this to me, now."

She sniffed and wiped her tears. "The class was practicing the song we were going to sing for the mother/daughter dance..." she sniffed again. "...just because my teacher said I was doing it right, those girls started laughing that they don't care how good I was singing, because I still don't have a mummy to sing the song to."

I let out a sigh of defeat and signed the document. "So, what did you yell?"

"I told them to shut up."

"You can't always—"

She stomped her feet. "But it's not fair, Daddy. Why don't I have a mummy? Mia has one, Ava has one. Why not me? Then when those girls tease me, and I stand up for myself I get in trouble."

I watched the agony on her face and hated myself. I really put my own feelings of fear above my daughter's need. As I walked over to Uju and lifted her onto the kitchen island, I thought about the conversation I had with my mother last night. She told me about some lady who had recently returned to Enugu from London. According to her, she'd be a good candidate for a wife. I listened, but didn't put too much thought into it as my mind was set on wooing Zola.

However, I no longer had the luxury of time to rely on the potential of a relationship with Zola that also had an uncertain future. Uju needed the stability of a mother in her life sooner rather than later. I walked over to dampen a paper towel and wiped my daughter's face. I then drew her into a hug and reassured her that everything would be okay. I made a mental note to text my sister to do her own background work on the woman my mother talked about. For my baby's peace of mind, I would marry her tomorrow if I had to.

Several minutes later, I was in the drop-off line when my phone buzzed.

Onyi: I got it brother, investigate her but don't tell mama.

I nodded at my sister's response. I had texted my assignment for her earlier. However, I needed to make sure she understood not to alert my mother. Just in case the woman didn't check out, I didn't want any unnecessary pressure on my neck. I had enough to deal with already. Sending her my appreciation, I replaced my phone in the holder. I had just dropped Uju and was now headed to my office. With any luck, this day would end on a higher note than how it started.

A light tap on my office door got me to lift my eyes from the email that currently had me grinding my teeth. My receptionist popped her head in when I granted permission. I took a deep breath, trying to shake off the irritation that had been building up inside me all day. Nothing irked me more than when my materials were delayed. For the last two years, the supply chain had been messed up. That's why I put in extra time. Still folks were trying to play with my time.

"Mr. Kalu, a Ms. Westbrook is here to see you."

I reclined in my chair and joined my index fingers together beneath my chin. The last I'd seen Zola was two days ago at Uju's dance recital. She had been much more amiable then, almost friendly even, sending me a few smiles—which I could tell were forced—but with the presence of other parents and their children, I chose not to confront her.

"Send her in."

"That's my cue. Don't forget, City Hall next Tuesday." Raven stood to leave. She'd stopped by to discuss an upcoming opportunity with the city.

Raven Collins was the recently appointed chairlady of the Arts & Culture committee for the city. We met at a function some years ago and developed a great working relationship that I could tell from her body language she now wanted to be more. Mixing business and pleasure was a huge no go for me and I preferred the business she brought rather than being the object of her pleasure. After I reassured her I'd be there, she opened the door.

On the opposite side, mid knock, stood the woman who invaded my thoughts. Zola walked in, both women briefly acknowledging each other. I banked the exchange in my mental Rolodex. Zola had claws. I liked that.

With my hands interlocked behind my head, I watched with hooded eyes as Zola moved closer to me. She was clad in a black turtleneck over black pants that hugged her curves in all the right places, made visible by the grey and black plaid coat that hung over her shoulders.

Our intense gazes remained locked as she neared my desk. I stood and walked to meet her.

"Mr. Kalu, I—"

"Nah, we not even about to do that. If you're going to waltz your fine self into my office without an appointment, that means we're past that. Let's try again." I stared at her until her stubbornness caved to my demand.

She shifted, exhaling a subtle sigh. "Jidenna, I'm sorry to interrupt—"

I moved to take her coat. "It's fine." When I noticed her chest rise and fall at my closeness, I flashed her a smile and gestured to the two chairs in front of my desk. "Have a seat." She walked over and took one while I carefully draped her coat over the other.

"To what do I owe the pleasure?" I leaned against my desk.

She looked up at me. "Can you sit down?"

I smirked. "Do I make you nervous, Zola?"

"No." The dip of her brows was cute.

"Liar."

"Whatever. Can you sit?"

"If you smile, I'll think about it."

I wasn't stupid. Her being here told me she wanted something. Despite my efforts, she'd been adamant about not having anything to do with me. Again, I can't say I blamed her, but I could no longer run behind her. Uju's tear-stricken face changed everything.

She flashed a phony smile that displayed all her thirty-two.

"Cute. But not good enough. I have all day, baby."

Our stand-off lasted all but a few seconds before she rolled her eyes and gave me what I wanted. It didn't quite reach her eyes, but it was good enough. I decided to give her the space I could sense she needed, walking behind my desk, I sat.

She cleared her throat and began to relay the reason she was here. As I listened to her talk about her father being in a financial bind, I thought she was here to ask for money. That got me tight, but then she began to talk about the masks I recently bought. She wanted me to let her father broker the deal between me and the sponsors of an upcoming exhibit in New York. It was the same one my sister asked me about a few months ago – the Global Connect people.

My jaw locked as she spouted off the talking points her father probably gave her. I felt a searing wave of anger wash all over me. I wasn't sure which made me angrier—the fact that her father would place her in this position, or the fact that she only came to see me because she needed something.

It was obvious Zola didn't want to be here. That was a fact she probably let her father know, but to clean up his mess, he disregarded her feelings and sent her here anyway.

"Your father could've reached out to me, but you are here. So

I'm assuming you know my stance, but want me to make an exception." My eyes held her captive.

"I know how this looks… bad. But I wouldn't be here if I really didn't have to," she pleaded.

"Bad? Nah…to ignore me until you needed something… forget bad. Baby, it looks terrible."

She stood, her fangs out, ready for war.

I took her in. For some insane reason, her annoyance stirred nerve endings in me that had no business being awakened.

"Are your little feelings hurt? Ever heard of 'what's good for the goose is good for the gander?'" She began to pace in front of my desk. "I can't believe you have the nerve to sit there and talk about being ignored. We went out and had…"

She stopped short, but I knew what she wanted to say because now I could admit it too.

One of the most memorable nights of our lives…

I felt the heat radiating off her and I tried to push my growing desire to pin her against the wall while my lips forced her body to admit what she refused to confess. I knew I wasn't right, but I didn't care. The vision I had of our tongues in a tug of war was interrupted when she banged her hands on my desk.

"Are you even listening to me?" she hissed. "You know what? Never mind."

She reached for her coat, and I was on her before she could touch it. Caging her between the desk and my body, I lifted her face with my index finger. I'd apologized before, but she blew me off. Now, I needed her to hear me. Fiery Zola did something to me I hadn't experienced in a while. And even though I loved her in my presence giving me a piece of her mind, I needed to erase the hurt underneath her anger.

"Look at me."

She ignored me and kept her eyes closed. Her breath snagged as she struggled to maintain control. I understood her plight as my chest burned with an agonizing ache as her scent crashed into me like a tidal wave that threatened to pull me under. Zola and I were a dangerous combination. My desire to possess her was potent and the reason I stayed away.

"Zola, look at me."

Her eyes met mine. Gone was the fire of seconds earlier. "It was never my intention to hurt you. Frankly, I didn't expect our night to turn out the way it did. The intensity of my attraction to you and our connection threw me for a loop and awakened things I had long since buried. But none of those reasons excuse blowing you off and not being truthful with you. I am sorry." I stared into her eyes. No matter what she came here for, I needed her to feel the sincerity of my apology.

As I spoke, I realized I also needed her to accept my apology. I didn't want to be a man synonymous with hurt for her. I wasn't sure if I would ever give my heart to anyone again. I'd always have love for Eno, but my stance wasn't about lingering feelings for her. This was about protecting myself from the pain associated with love. My cousins called me a punk, but the pain that came with loss had to be experienced to be understood.

A grin spread across her face, and I braced myself for the bull that was about to come out of her mouth. "So, what I'm hearing is…you…" She jabbed her finger at me. "…Mr. 'Famous Artist who maintains a habitual scowl because we peasants don't deserve his smile' Kalu…is scared of little ol' me?"

I reared my head back and laughed. That beautiful smile I wanted to keep on her face resurfaced. A real one this time. I leaned in close to her ears. "You should be scared of me too."

She placed a hand on my chest to push me back. Deciding to give her the space she needed, I stepped back a little. "Nah, buddy. I need you to admit it."

"If I do, will you forgive me?"

"Maybe."

I frowned.

"I'll seriously consider it."

"Not good enough."

"How are you going to force me into accepting your apology?"

"The same way you thought coming in here trying to use your charm on me would have me bending to your will."

"Fair." She placed her hand on her hip. "So?" Her eyes darted to the framed picture of my daughter on the desk. "She's so adorable."

"She thinks highly of you too, Teach." I winked at her.

"Not you too. Your cousin is enough."

I chuckled, raising my hands in surrender. Cheta dropped in briefly for Uju's Twirl with Dad dance routine on Friday. It was amusing watching him tease Zola about running away from the gang. To which she promptly replied that she was kicked out. Cheta, of course, acted shocked then promised to avenge any wrongdoing she might have endured.

"Back to the matter at hand," I said, trying to get us back on course.

"Will you agree to my request?" she asked.

"You mean your father's request."

"No, my request to help my dad."

"Semantics, baby." I tucked a loose tress behind her ear. "But both issues are mutually exclusive. Let's handle one before the other."

"Okay, I forgive you."

"Not convinced."

"Jidennaaa..."

"I love fiery Zola, but I think I might like pleading Zola better."

"You're about to get violent Zola. I forgive you. I promise. I mean it's not your fault all this..." She gestured at her body. "...had you running for the hills."

"Third strike and I'm taking you out."

"Do tell. How?" She hiked her brow.

"Are you bold enough to find out?"

She contemplated for a few more seconds before deciding to find something safe to do. "No."

"Hmmm. Okay, now to your father. I'll do you one better."

"Explain."

"I'll agree to a two-year lease, with my team handling the installation. Transportation, insurance, and any other expenses are handled by your father and or the sponsor – I don't really care which." I took a breath because what I was about to ask for in return was no different than the position her father put her in. However, she was as attracted to me as I was to her, so I was sure that my ask was going to be less uncomfortable.

Zola squinted at me. "That wasn't so hard. I thought I was going to have to grovel or fight."

I lifted my brow. "Nothing's off the table yet."

She giggled. "Still, thank you. That's so genero—"

"Hold on a sec." I watched her brows dip and felt an unease at putting a damper on her mood, but I pushed through. "I'd love to help you out, but I need—"

"Okay, I'll go out with you."

"I appreciate it, but we're past that." She remained silent, so I continued. "I need you to marry me."

She laughed nervously and walked in a circle in front of me. I folded my arms across my chest and leaned against my desk. My eyes followed her movement, as she paced, shaking her head, and mumbling something to herself. She stopped in front of me and studied my expression. I noticed the moment it dawned on her that I was serious. After this morning's incident with Uju, I was open to marrying a total stranger so she would have a mother. But as Zola was speaking, something clicked for me. Why marry a total stranger when I could marry a semi-stranger that I was deeply attracted to as I knew she was to me?

"Wait what? Why would I marry you when you ghosted me for months? What about love? This is ridiculous. I heard your explanation about being scared, but what has changed?"

"What's changed is you need this for your family, and I need a mother for my daughter. Besides, love alone does not sustain a marriage – commitment does." I allowed my words to sink in before continuing. "Also, I'm now ready to see what we can become, but only as your husband." I placed my hands on her hip and drew her closer to me, parking her between my legs. She sucked in a breath.

"Can't we do this another way? I can be there for her if–"

"That's the deal, Zola. You need something and so do I. I've seen you with Uju on multiple occasions; she adores you. She needs stability, a nurturing mother figure and you get... by my rough calculations, ten million dollars. For your father, of course."

She sucked her teeth, squirming in my embrace.

"I didn't mean it like that, but it is what it is. We're adults who are attracted to each other, so the deal comes with added benefits." I rose to my full height, not letting go of her waist.

I moved in closer, lowering my head. I allowed my mouth to hover over hers and her eyes unexpectedly closed in anticipation of what was to come. My lips brushed against her soft ones, causing a warm sensation and energy that was enough to send a jolt through my entire body. My method of persuasion wasn't purely selfish as I planned to give her an equally satisfying experience.

I cupped Zola's face, pulling her closer to me as I hungrily took control of her mouth. My tongue invaded the crevices, searching for satisfaction only she could provide. Sensing her eagerness, I deepened our connection, weaving my fingers in her hair. I felt her hands exploring my sides, clutching at my shirt. After a few passionate moments, I drew back, ending our tango. Her eyelids fluttered before her eyes locked with mine, leaving us in a heavy trance. I peppered several more kisses on her lips before relinquishing control.

Zola's eyes narrowed before turning into slits. I suppressed a grin because her anger wasn't with me, but with her body's response to me. The betrayal had her about to blow. Choosing to maintain her silence, she flung her coat across her arm, picked up her bag and stalked toward the door, yanking it open with more force than necessary.

"I'll let you think about it. But don't take too long, baby. You did say time was of the essence," I called out.

Zola's eyes flicked to mine with a vexed expression before she stormed out of the room, her heels clicking against the mosaic floor. The scent of jasmine from her perfume lingered in the air as I let myself digest what had just happened.

My lips curved into a smile as I walked back to my seat. Although I didn't have her answer yet, I was feeling lucky since the day had turned out better than expected.

"Nah, not luck," I muttered.

According to my grandmother, there was no such thing as luck, but the divine will of God.

8

ZOLA

"So, you're really about to become this man's wife."

Staring at the six-carat, oval halo engagement ring on my finger, I responded. "In exactly six hours." An April bride. *This wasn't on my bingo card for the year.* Who would have thought it?

Jidenna went all out for this ring. A week after my visit to his office, I called him to agree on our arrangement. He invited me out for dinner the next day. When he arrived at my home carrying a bouquet of flowers, I couldn't help but smile in admiration as he stood in my living room and took in my space. As I headed to get my purse, I stared at him in his African print outfit. He wore regular clothes sometimes, but I was a sucker for when he dressed in traditional garb.

His black fabric with red embroidery was beautiful and he finished it off with his signature hat and black loafers. I had no prior knowledge of what he was going to wear, but I was glad my sequined, off-the-shoulder black dress and red clutch matched his fly. We had an enjoyable evening at an upscale restaurant, and our conversation flowed easily. I wanted to stay distant and angry about him ghosting me, but I couldn't.

"This isn't conventional. But this part, I'm going to do right."

Before I could ask him what he meant, Jidenna took my hand and got down on one knee.

"Zola Amoy Westbrook, I may not be able to guarantee an easy journey or perfection. But I can promise that every day I will choose to honor my commitment to you and my daughter. To protect and provide until my last breath. Will you do life with me and marry me?"

The soft music playing in the background combined with the candles and flowers had my throat clogged with emotion. For that one night, I imagined that our coming together wasn't an arrangement.

"And no one in your family knows?"

I lifted my eyes to Tessa, the memory scattering away like mist. We had just entered our top floor suite of the Walden Luxury Hotel & Casino in Las Vegas. The view of the city skyline was breathtaking. The hotel, owned by billionaire Darius Gray, was a beauty to behold. Everything was operated with smart technology. From the grand entrance to the refined decor, it was clear that no expense had been spared in creating the luxurious and exclusive establishment. I'd love to return under better circumstances, or at least enjoy it. But right now, the nervousness bubbling up in my belly prevented me from doing that.

"Tess, the answer isn't going to change from the last five times you've asked me this question." I strolled over to the nightstand and picked up the neatly folded card with "Soon to be Mrs. Kalu" written in neat cursive handwriting.

She raised her hands in surrender. "I'm making sure because your parents are going to flip, especially your mom." Gesturing toward my hand, she asked, "Is that from him?"

I nodded, but made no move to open the card. For reasons I couldn't explain, I wanted to savor its contents in private. "I'm keeping the dream alive, so I highly doubt they'll be too mad."

Slipping the card into my back pocket, I entered the closet to hang the outfit I'd be changing into later.

"Now, you know that them asking you to get Jidenna to change his mind about the masks, and you marrying him for the masks are two different things."

I did know that. However, considering the shame I'd brought to my family's name, I could at least do something to help my parents out. True, they would never agree if they knew, but after I thought about it long and hard, Jidenna did have a point. This would be mutually beneficial for both of us. A point I wasn't ready to admit to at first until my mother called a couple of days later.

She started off by asking about my progress with Jidenna, but before I could provide an answer, she informed me that the bank had sent appraisers over to the house. She was spitting fire telling me how embarrassed she was and that she was done with my dad. Before I could process that information, she informed me that she'd be coming to stay with me for a few weeks. She was angry that my father had put the family in this situation in the first place. Despite the united front they presented the last time I saw them, I knew my mother well enough to know that my dad's secrecy wasn't something she would get over so soon. Especially since the problem wasn't resolved. Her anxiety over the continued uncertainty of the situation would cause her to erupt at odd times, keeping the flame of acrimony between them alive.

To get her to calm down, I blurted out that Jidenna had agreed. Before I could utter another word, she squealed, yelling for my dad to come hear the good news. There was no turning back after that, so I got off the phone, waited a few days then called Jidenna.

The lazy way in which he answered the phone irritated me because he knew I would call. His arrogant tone made me want to reach through the phone and lay hands on him, but at the same time weirdly turned me on. Jidenna agreed to meet with my dad *after* we were married. Since we had a little over a week left before the bank came calling, here I was three days later.

"Tess, it's happening. I need your support. Please." I plopped down on the bed.

After a long exhale, she pushed off the dresser she was leaning against and squatted in front of me. "Okay, real talk. Nobody knows me better than you and I'd like to think the same applies with me—"

"It does." My eyes misted.

"If I thought for one moment you were entering into an arrangement that will have you miserable, I'd go to war to stop you." Tessa thumbed away the tear that formed at the corner of my eye. "I saw you with Caleb and although you loved him, watching you and Jidenna at lunch earlier was like watching a wildfire engulfing everything in its path. My only issue is that while I know you love him—"

"I don't!" I protested, my voice not even strong enough to hold the argument.

Tessa waved me off. "Sis, you're in denial because of your anger and that's fine. But like I was saying, while I know you love him, I'm not sure he's there yet. So, please make this whatever you want it to be, but see things for what they are and not what you want them to be."

Tessa stood and drew me up. We embraced in a long hug I desperately needed. Since the day I woke up to my parents fighting over the family's financial status, I felt like I had been reeling in emotions, drowning in a burden I wished I didn't have to bear.

Tessa was right. I did love Jidenna. Before the night of the gala, we'd engaged in light conversation from time to time. The gala and the time we spent together awakened something in me. I mean, I'd heard all the cheesy love at first sight stories, but I never believed them. Over the next several months, I hated myself for not being able to erase him from my mind. Then for him to waltz back into my life seemed like a bad joke. But despite it all, I wanted to be with him, but that was something I wasn't ready to admit aloud.

While Tessa walked into the bathroom, I opened the note. My eyes glossed over the neatness of his script.

> *Olaedo m (my jewel),*
>
> *Let's make this day unforgettable, something we will forever savor and treasure in our hearts. Can't wait to see you, beautiful. JDK*

Placing the note on my chest, I allowed myself to wander to a dreamy place of possibilities before succumbing to sleep.

A few hours later, Tessa had me twirl. I smiled, shook my head, and did her bidding.

"When you wanted to go for this outfit, I wasn't sure, but sis, that man won't know whether to say his vows or lie you at the altar."

When I got married the first time, I had the perfect princess wedding that every little girl dreamed of. The dress was a mermaid cut that had a train and veil that was almost three feet long. The décor was something from a fairy-tale, the food was incredible, there was a live band; it was everything. However, despite all the expense, the marriage ended quickly. Now at thirty-one, I was a grown woman, and I didn't need the hoopla. I was the one that suggested we fly to Las Vegas to do this. But I was a Westbrook, so things might be simple but would be classy.

To my surprise, earlier, Jidenna sent a masseuse to work out all my kinks. Without me saying anything, he knew I was stressed. That melted my heart. I was tickled when a woman showed up. As she was setting up, I sent him a text thanking him, but teasing him that "she" wasn't a "he." I cackled when I got his response saying, "I'm trying to be married, not end up in jail."

After the massage, I took a shower and soon the hair and makeup folks showed up. I stared at my reflection in the full-length, silver-frame mirror. The white, feathery fabric of my tube top jumpsuit hugged my curves, and my hair was in a low bun with a few strands cascading down the side of my lightly beat face. In my ears were pearl studs, accented by silver hoops. I sucked in a breath, feeling the nerves of this next step build within me and prayed to God it worked out in my favor. Deep down, I knew that despite my denial, I did love Jidenna. I hoped he'd catch up to me soon. If not, I was in for a lonely ride.

～

"Hey, let me talk to you for a minute."

Without waiting for an answer, Jidenna grabbed my hand and dragged me away from Tessa as we entered the lobby of the chapel.

"Uhhhh…excuse you," Tessa said.

He gave her a salute. "My bad, Tessa. I need to talk to my wife real quick."

"Oh gosh. He's about to 'my wife' us to death," Tessa teased.

I giggled.

"That's what she's about to be, ain't it?" Jidenna asked while his eyes gave me a once over.

"I ain't mad at it. But like I told you before, I got hands."

"Your girl is good in his. Let's allow the couple to have a few words," Jidenna's friend, David, said.

Earlier during lunch, Jidenna introduced David to me as one of the few college friends he kept in contact with over the years. David lived in Las Vegas and worked in real estate.

I heard David and Tessa bickering as we walked toward the opposite side of the chapel. When we talked about coming to Las Vegas to get married quickly, Jidenna and I agreed against telling our families. Even Uju wasn't here. I didn't like that, but we agreed that telling them and the questions that would ensue would take up time we didn't have. We were already cutting it close with the time it took for funds transfer. So, instead of his cousins, he decided to bring one of his friends to stand with Tessa as a witness. Knowing my mother, there would be a time for whatever celebration she wanted to have, but that time wasn't now.

"You good?" Jidenna asked once we were in the corner of the chapel.

"If I'm not, will you call off the wedding?" I joked, knowing I was reaching. The deal we had was a wife for his change of policy with the masks.

"That's not an option. However, I do have other ways to make you feel better." He placed his hands on my hips. "You look beautiful by the way." He kissed my forehead.

"Thanks. I'm fine. You don't look too bad yourself."

My eyes raked over his appearance. As usual, Jidenna stood tall and proud with that hint of Nigerian arrogance. His black tuxedo had a velvety texture that looked smooth to the touch. Matching leather oxfords covered his feet. The scent of his cologne filled my nostrils, reminding me of the danger of being wrapped up in his orbit. He was without his signature hat, allowing me to admire the waves of his low-cut hair.

"This isn't ideal, but I do care about you. I want you to know that this can be whatever we want it to be. I'll follow your lead."

"I appreciate you saying that. And I'll hold up my end of the deal. But I could've mentored JuJu for free." I winked at him.

"Too bad she doesn't need a mentor. She needs a mother and I need a wife. Nice try though." He pulled me closer, and I chuckled.

"A'ight y'all, it's time." David's voice caused both our heads to turn.

Jidenna grabbed my hand, kissed the back of it and led us to the front of the chapel. For the first time, I looked around the chapel. The inviting space was adorned with soft, twinkling fairy lights and delicate candlelight. It was a romantic and intimate atmosphere, in a strange way, perfect for the day. After the final instructions by the attendant, Tessa squeezed my hand and handed me the bouquet. The chorus of "The Best Part" by H.E.R ft. Daniel Caesar started to play as I walked down the aisle to a waiting Jidenna. I teared up.

He remembered.

All these months I thought he forgot about me, my husband to be remembered.

Once I got to him, I handed off my bouquet to Tessa while Jidenna took my hands in his. Everything after that was a haze. An electric shock ran through me as we locked eyes. The officiant seemed to hum in the background as the ceremony began. Our vows flew by in a blur, then it came time for us to exchange rings, solidifying our commitment to each other. The moment that would forever be etched in my mind was when Jidenna drew me close, and we kissed with intense passion.

A few hours later, we were back in the VIP area of the hotel lounge. The four of us ate, laughed, and danced. The circumstances that brought us together disappeared as Jidenna and I couldn't keep our hands off each other, savoring each moment. Our chemistry was a non-issue; keeping a grip on our emotions was going to be the tricky part. By morning, reality would step in, so for now I wanted to relish the feeling of being held by my husband, within our own little bubble.

Twenty-one days. Five hundred and four hours. Thirty thousand, two hundred and forty minutes.

Three weeks...

That's how long it'd been since I became a wife, mother, and moved into my new home. Jidenna and I were getting used to being married - bickering over the little things, like setting the thermostat temperature, choosing which shows to watch, or reconciling his morning persona against my nighttime one. Even so, we had similar principles at heart, so I knew that all the other issues would get resolved soon enough. The time had gone by so quickly, yet it felt like a lifetime of emotions all crammed into the brief period. Tessa, Jidenna, and I flew back to Atlanta the morning after our nuptials. When we arrived at Jidenna's house, Uju was still asleep. Waking her up, we broke the news to her together. I wasn't sure whether it was because I'd been in her life for almost three years or the fact that, like Jidenna said, she needed a mother, but the little girl jumped for joy, hugging me to the point of almost cutting off my air supply.

I had heard of stories of girls being extremely territorial over their fathers, but her attitude was the total opposite. Apart from the brief scowl on her face when she questioned the validity of our marriage, or when she needed clarification of our living arrangements before demanding my promise not to leave her like her *other* mommy, Uju didn't show any major displeasure to the news. Satisfied with my response, she turned to her father. Jidenna asked her again if she was okay. After she confirmed she was, he pulled her into a tight embrace and they both expressed their love for each other. It was a beautiful sight to behold.

Moments later, Uju floated down the hallway back to her room. Stopping at the door, she asked if she could tell other people. It seemed like the little girl had been floating on air ever since.

On the other hand, saving my family's name also solidified my place as the prodigal daughter. I picked up the toothbrush and used a little edge control gel to smooth Uju's edges. In a few minutes, we'd be headed to Luxe Noir. I rubbed the center of my chest, trying to ease the dull ache brought on by my accelerated heart rate. I was really dreading the next two days. I seriously prayed everything would go well.

Unlike the Kalus whose initial shock turned into a comedy show with zinging jokes before they congratulated us, my parents were livid at our rushed nuptials. Although, my dad, Jidenna and their respective teams had communicated over many virtual meetings in the days after our return from Las Vegas, there was a palpable tension between my dad and Jidenna.

For my dad, I think it was more his wounded ego. He kept talking about Jidenna forcing me to marry him without asking his permission. On the other hand, my mom was angry about me acting without thinking. She was worried about what assumptions the town would make at such a rushed wedding. Deep down though, I could also sense her worry about our differences. However, at no time did either of my parents demand I get the marriage annulled with their reassurance they would find another way to get the money.

To both families, we met, settled our differences, and decided to get married. That was our story and the truth without minor details. In the back of my mind, I knew his cousins didn't think Jidenna was in love with me, however, I was sure he didn't tell them about the masks and my family's financial troubles. Before leaving Las Vegas, he looked me in the eye and promised he would never share that with another soul. I believed him.

"I like it, Ms. Zola." Uju turned her head from side to side, using her bathroom mirror to inspect the job I'd done.

"You're welcome, darling. Now which dress did you choose?"

I followed Uju to her bed. With her finger on her lips in contemplation, she looked between both dresses we'd picked out earlier. I folded my arms over my chest, amused at how mature she acted sometimes. The first few days after I moved in, I found myself consulting Jidenna any time I wanted to engage with Uju.

After initially reassuring me that he trusted me, he had to finish with a touch of sarcasm. "Besides, you're now her mother...mother her."

Moments later, Uju had decided on a dress, slipped on her

shoes, and followed me to my room. Jidenna and I shared the master bedroom, but he didn't sleep in it. There has been so much going on that we hadn't gotten to that part of our relationship. The pent-up sexual energy was there, in his eyes, touch, and words. We kissed and made out here and there, but we hadn't made love. Even though somedays I wanted to jump him and demand my pleasure, I knew he was right and agreed when he said we should wait until things settled a bit.

"We're locked in, baby. That will come, but first I wanna get to know your mind," he'd said.

However, since we were modelling a healthy relationship for Uju, Jidenna went to the guest room only when she fell asleep.

Uju sat on the bed while I walked into the closet. Our bags were packed for our two-day stay. All I needed was to change and put on some lipstick before Jidenna came back upstairs, threatening to leave us behind for the third time.

"I'm so glad you are my mommy, Ms. Zola," Uju said.

I smiled taking my dress off the hanger. "I'm honored to be your mommy. But remember what we talked about…"

"Yes. I won't forget my first mommy who went to be with Jesus."

"Yes, she loved you so much, but she had to leave. I love you too, and I'll try to be the best bonus mommy to you." Dressed, I strolled out of the closet and placed a kiss on her forehead before walking over to my vanity.

"You look pretty. I knew my daddy liked you."

"Your daddy liked me huh?" My eyes met Uju's in the mirror. "Tell me more."

She giggled. "I told him that he looks at you like boys on the TV look at girls they want to—"

"JuJu, what I tell you about spilling family secrets?" Jidenna entered the room. His eyes roamed my body while he walked over to the bed toward Uju.

"But Ms. Zola is family, so we can tell her. Right Daddy?"

He pulled her up from the bed and twirled her. "You look pretty, my princess."

"Thank you, Daddy. Ms. Zola is family, right Daddy?"

"Yeah, I'm family, right *Daddy?*" I picked up my necklace and smiled at the warning his eyes gave me.

Jidenna sauntered over to me and took the necklace from my hand. His gaze held mine captive in the mirror as he put the necklace on. Leaning closer to me, his cool breath which carried a mix of mint and menthol sent a shiver down my spine.

"Don't think for one second, I won't shut this trip down and show you what *Daddy* does to his naughty queen. Don't play with fire, baby." He kissed my neck and stepped back. "You look beautiful."

My word of gratitude was stuck in my throat, so I smiled and walked over to take Uju's hand. "We're ready."

"Good, let's be out."

As we got to the door, I stopped and turned to him. "You promised you'd be good."

"You know I've shown a lot of restraint, but I made you a promise. Stop worrying."

We left the room. Honestly, he was right. My dad had come at him sideways too many times and I knew that the alpha in him showed restraint because of me. Jidenna did try to apologize for not asking for my hand in marriage from my dad. That totally shocked me. Still my dad dragged out his displeasure. My mom pleaded for us to come this weekend. I prayed she cautioned her husband like I asked because if disrespected, I wouldn't be able to stop the wrath of mine.

9

JIDENNA

Her eyes conveyed her plea.

Remembering the look my wife gave me before I followed her father to his study a few minutes ago was the only thing keeping the thread of restraint I had from being completely severed. Unlike my cousin, Cheta, I tried to hold on to my temper because when I lost it, putting it back in the bottle wasn't always easy. Besides I couldn't let my girls see me like that.

"I'm sure you understand I wanted better for my daughter," Mr. Westbrook said.

Before speaking, I allowed my eyes to roam the impeccably styled room. The opulence of the space was marked by intricate carvings on the wall, the drapes, and the plush leather furniture.

"As a father myself, I understand that you have certain expectations for your daughter," I replied evenly. My voice barely masked the anger simmering below the surface. "The speed in which we came together was something we both decided on. My parents had the same concern. But as I told them and I'm telling you…again, she is in good hands. We care about each other deeply and I give you my word that I'll do everything in my power to make her happy."

Two days after Zola and I returned from Las Vegas, I walked in on Zola on the phone with her parents, giving her flack about our marriage. I'd walked in through the garage and the earthy, sweet, nutty scent of oatmeal cookies floated up my nostrils. I smiled recalling her and Uju discussing their baking plans the night before. Almost immediately, my light mood gave way to anger when I neared the kitchen and saw her rubbing her temples listening to her parents.

My first instinct was to hang up her phone. But those eyes again begged me to hold on. So I did, until I couldn't. Walking out of the kitchen, I tried to suppress my anger as I headed to my daughter's room to inquire about her day.

The next day, I called Mr. Westbrook and conveyed my regrets for not informing him of my intent to marry his daughter. Considering his bruised ego, that was the second courtesy I'd given. This was now the third and definitely the last. It wouldn't even be happening if he hadn't asked to speak to me in private. I found it amusing how I was good enough to save his status among his friends, but not good enough to marry his daughter. Whatever his problem was, he needed to deal with it because this wasn't about to be a regular occurrence. No one else was going to question me. Not even my own father.

"I didn't hear you mention love. Do you love my daughter, or did you see our business as an opportunity and go for it? Business is business, but tying my daughter—"

I stood, set my drink down and shoved my fisted hands in my pocket, giving myself time to cool down.

"You keep throwing around your *daughter* title. I got one that trumps that...*my wife*. For three weeks, I've watched her in anguish because of your displeasure. For her, I've tried to appeal to you, explain even." I thumbed my nose when I saw his jaw clench. "Explaining is something I don't do. It would make my wife happy if we got along, but let me remind you, that is a grown woman who I'm now responsible for. Make no mistake, I will cut off anyone and anything that threatens her peace." I paused, allowing my words to sink in.

"Despite this mishap, I admire what you've built here, sir. However, since you sent your *daughter* to me, you also know who and what I am. You don't have to like me, but I won't stand for disrespect."

Going back and forth with anybody wasn't something I did. Even the women I entertained prior could never get an argument out of me. My nonchalance got on their nerves. The only person I now gave any energy to was the woman I'd given my last name. Done with this conversation, I needed to go look for my girls.

A few hours later, I stood on the wooden deck of the large, covered patio, listening to my contractor explain the logistics delaying the extension I was having built on my Enugu home. Growing up with money, few things impressed me, but the West-brook estate was a sight to behold. The views from the back of the property were as spectacular as the front. The mansion was surrounded by lush green gardens and had an astonishing view of the town's horizon.

A long winding paved driveway led up to the three-story home with cream colored stone for its exterior. The gated entrance had a gold "W" on it and was nestled in between two large, majestic trees. The entire estate was surrounded by tall and flourishing hedges, making it feel like a secluded paradise. As an artist, I had a deeper admiration for nature's beauty.

Earlier, Zola gave me a brief rundown of its history. Nothing compared to seeing it up close. I was eager to visit the community center Zola talked about. She explained that her family had another home on the island, but since her parents' offices were in town, they spent most of the time here.

When we first arrived, Zola's dad wasn't home, but her mother was. Two of her brothers were out of the country, one was out of town while her last brother and sister would be joining us for brunch the following day.

Mrs. Westbrook's elegance reminded me of Arinze's mother, Aunty Bola. We all called Aunty B the fashionista of the family because she almost never wore the same thing twice. At first, Mrs. Westbrook was a little cold, but my wife must've said something to her because she warmed up to me in no time. I wasn't feeling her though. If it took someone to say something to you to be nice to me, then you could forget it. However, the frost I had for her melted as I watched her interactions with Uju. You could do anything to me, but my daughter? I'd never play about her. After asking me the normal questions a mother would ask, she and my girls headed to the kitchen as her father arrived.

After that little chat we had, we all sat down for lunch. My wife kept trying to get me to tell her what happened, but I wouldn't budge. I'd either kiss her forehead or squeeze her hand, reassuring her that everything was fine. I guess Mrs. Westbrook had a chat with her husband because he was a different man from the one I left in the study. We weren't chummy, but I had knocked the block off his shoulder.

"Tony, this is unacceptable. I'll be there in a few weeks, and I want that place done," I said. I hated incompetence with every fiber of my being. Cutting him off when he tried to make another empty promise, I reiterated my annoyance with the situation. In the middle of my tirade, a hand moved around my stomach. I sensed her approach before I saw her.

Ending the call, I pulled Zola to my front. Her eyes widened, a hint of amusement flickering in them as I leaned down to capture her lips in a possessive kiss. Zola moaned into my mouth, her fingers digging into my shoulders as I walked her back to the wicker chair before breaking the kiss and pulling her into my lap.

"You do know this is my parent's house?" she asked, swatting my chest while adjusting herself for better comfort.

"You're the one feeling up all on me. Besides, you're mine, so I can do what I want when I want."

"Cocky much?"

"Nah, just spitting facts." I turned my head to the double doors. "Where is JuJu?"

Zola giggled. "Touring my mother's garden. I knew she missed her grandkids, but I didn't know how much until I saw her with Ju."

"I'm happy they're enjoying themselves. What about you? You good?" I saw her and her dad talking earlier. I didn't notice any tension between them, but I still wanted to be sure.

"I'm fine. You know your overprotectiveness is cute."

"Ain't nothing cute about me, baby. I protect my own. Any man that can't do that isn't worth the time."

"I'll make sure I put that on the top of my criteria list next time." With a smirk, she stuck out her tongue at me.

"Right after that, put pick out the dress you want to wear to his funeral."

Zola laughed. She might think I was joking, but wasn't nothing funny about the thought of her and the next man.

"That goes both ways, buddy."

"Without question."

"Anyway, your overprotectiveness is sexy," she said, as I pushed her hair back from her face. "So, can I convince you to protect me and Ju, here, tonight?"

"Nice try, but I'm not staying here with you and Ju. My double suite at the Regal Oasis has more than enough space for the three of us if you wanna stay with me." There was no way I could sleep under her parents' roof. That was a cultural thing I wasn't bending on.

"Oh, come on husband, won't you miss us?"

"That should never be a question." I kissed her nose. "But it's one night. We leave tomorrow afternoon."

"I guess. So where are you taking me tonight?"

"Is your mom good with watching Ju?"

"Of course." She frowned. "Why wouldn't she be?"

"I'on know." I shrugged. "Maybe she had plans. I don't know what people with money do on a Saturday night."

"Very funny. But yes, so where are we going?"

"It's your town. Where you wanna go?"

"Hmm, there is this restaurant called Roots & Rhythms. The food is divine. I haven't been there in a while."

I tapped her thigh. "Okay, then." She stood and so did I. "Let me get to the hotel, make a few calls, and rest a bit. I'll be back to get you by 7."

With her hand in mine, I walked us to the door. "You remember I leave for Chicago Monday?"

"Yeah, I remember. So I guess the honeymoon phase is over."

My wife and I were still getting to know each other. The speed of the wedding, amid meetings with her father and his people, then with my staff about transportation of the pieces, to getting my wife moved and settled in, we were left with no time to spend quality time with each other. There was still a lot I wanted to know about Zola, and tonight I planned on starting that process.

"That part hasn't even started. We're in the prelude." I squeezed her waist, and she rewarded me with the smile I'd come to crave.

"You know it's funny, I grew up here and although I came here with my folks, I've never experienced it like I have tonight."

Tucking her hair, I brushed my lips against my wife's neck. Her head was on my chest as we lounged on the deck of the yacht. We both had physical touch as our dominant love language, so she was always on me, and I wasn't complaining in the least.

When I got back to my suite earlier, I looked into the restaurant she told me about, Roots & Rhythms. It was an upscale traditional Afro-Caribbean restaurant on the marina. We had the option of dining on the water or in the restaurant. I chose the water and it cost a pretty penny to rent out the small yacht. However, it was worth every moment of the peace and serenity we had.

"I'm glad you liked it."

The salty tang of the sea fused with the aroma of the Afro-Caribbean cuisine lingered in the air. Zola and I had both opted for jerk chicken with rice and peas. Jerk wasn't as spicy as the food I normally ate, but it was what my wife recommended, and it was a good choice. This dish wasn't like the one I was used to. The artistic plating and garnishes got me first, enhancing the appeal. The dish itself, as explained by the waiter, was made with locally sourced ingredients which were used to craft a marinade that highlighted the nuanced flavors of the spices and peppers. He told no lies.

Over dinner, the conversation flowed smoothly. I wasn't sure if it was subconsciously done, but neither of us talked about expectations of the marriage. Instead, we shared our likes, dislikes, hobbies, and how we got started in our careers before landing on her infamous backpacking trip across Europe.

I teased her because although our upbringings were similar in terms of money, the Kalu brothers would never allow their sons backpack through Europe or anywhere for a year. My cousins and I got side eyes as it were for not being doctors, lawyers, and engineers, but more than that, for not joining the family business. I was an engineer, but I didn't practice; so that was just as bad. Our seats on the board still didn't make up for our absences in our parents' opinion.

With my eyes trained on the sun setting over the water, casting an orange glow across the bay, I adjusted the blanket I had brought with us. Since I knew we would be dining on the water, I stopped at the gift shop in the hotel and bought a blanket. One of things I had found out about my wife was the fact that she was always cold. Our first night at home, she almost had me drowning in a pool of sweat with how hot she had the house. The next day, I was at her favorite store buying all textures of blankets and throws because it was not about to be a sauna in our home.

The sound of lapping waves and gentle music drifted towards us, creating a soothing, peaceful ambiance. My chest vibrated when I remembered something she had told me earlier about her European trip.

"Why are you laughing?" she asked.

"I can't believe you asked the people for a condom at eight in the morning."

She giggled and nudged me. "I did not. That French waiter heard what he wanted to hear. How does *capote* sound like *confiture*? I wanted jam. They should've known that. I had bread in front of me for goodness sake."

I laughed again. "And your friend is wild." Apparently, Tessa fueled the fire by telling the waiter that they also wanted a side of men.

"She always gets me in trouble."

"She only enhances the naughty that already exists."

"Aye! You're my husband. You're supposed to say nice things."

"Who says I don't like naughty?"

"Is that why you like Raven?"

Raven and my wife were like night and day. From the little I knew of Zola, she could get risky with her attire and had a feisty side, but she was also demure and chill when she needed to be. Every time I'd encountered Raven, she was on a hundred all the time. She knew her stuff, was beautiful and confident. I liked that. Every woman had their place. Raven's wasn't with me.

I sighed. "What you wanna know?"

"Nothing."

"Nah, I allowed you get away with that answer the first time you made a snarky comment. But here we are again. So…ask…"

Zola sat up and looked at me. "She doesn't work for you, so why is she always around?"

"Always is an exaggeration." I pinned her with my eyes. "However, she's leading an initiative for the city that I'm a part of. Also, a while ago, she helped me get JDK in the running for a bid with the High Museum." I studied her for a bit before adding. "That's strictly business."

"Does she know that?"

"I don't care what she knows. I know what I said and what it is." A few beats passed between us. "I want to enjoy the evening with my wife and not talk about anyone that doesn't matter."

Satisfied with my answer, she resumed her former position. I thought I was the possessive one, but my wife was something else. Of course, my ego loved it. Besides she looked so beautiful when she was worked up. Zola was far from insecure, but my first sighting of her in action was when we went to Uju's school. We were there to add her as Uju's mother and emergency contact. I'm sure the office clerk who got reckless with her hand over mine wouldn't forget that encounter anytime soon.

"Hmmm."

I kissed the top of her head. "I didn't say anything when what's his face claimed to be calling to congratulate you on your wedding."

I remembered the day my wife, I and Uju were in the kitchen preparing snacks for movie night and her phone rang with her ex on the line. She'd told me a little about the dude and I didn't like him off rip. For the mere fact that he had her before me. I should thank him for fumbling her, but she experienced pain as a result, and I wasn't thankful for that.

"Oh, sure. Not even when you made sure to yell out in the background that I was holding up movie night." She chuckled softly and snuggled closer to me.

I left a gentle kiss on top of her head. "I have no idea what you're talking about."

"Yeah, right. Anyway, I've been wanting to ask. If we're only going to Nigeria for your parent's anniversary and mom's birthday party, why are we staying for three weeks?"

"My wife doesn't wanna stay in my home with me?"

"Stop putting words in my mouth. I have a studio to run, remember? Then I need to prepare Ju for the new school year, and she's already told me about her birthday. I need to plan for all that."

"I love it when you mother, but we'll be in Enugu for only a week and a half, then you and I have other business."

Zola tried to sit up, but I didn't want to lose her warmth, so I held her closer. "You wanna share?"

"Nope. But moving on, you and your sister good now?"

Right before we arrived, Zola and her sister exchanged a few words about what she called her sneakiness lately. Zola explained that wasn't the case, but Zuri wasn't trying to hear it. Before our dessert arrived, Zola excused herself to call her sister back.

"Yeah, we're okay. It's always been this way. She claims I treat Tessa more like a sister than I do her. That's not the case at all, but I can see how this present situation reiterated her belief." She tried to sit and this time I let her. "Everything happened so fast, and I know she's under the stress of planning her wedding. I couldn't risk telling her anything."

"I see your point, but I also see hers. Family is important, so I'm glad you worked it out."

She ran her hand through her hair. "I still have my older sister, and my brothers Isaiah, Elijah, and Jeremiah to deal with. Noah, who you'll meet tomorrow, is my immediate older brother, but he's chill."

I raised my brow, and she held her index finger up. "Don't even say it. Yes, all prophet names, now moving on..."

I raised my hands and laughed. We already talked about the Z names for the girls. "Anyway, you know when it comes to you, my cape stays ready."

"Aww, how sweet, my personal superman."

Zola paused and I could feel her unease. "What's wrong?"

"The last time I got married, I was so sure I'd be with Caleb forever. I mean everything felt right. It was the quintessential love story." She seemed to be struggling with retelling the memories.

Although I wasn't beat for hearing her talk about her ex-husband, I knew she needed to get it out. "I know I was young, but I was so sure. So, in typical Westbrook fashion, my parents spared no expense for the wedding. Then two years later, the fairytale turned into a nightmare. The divorce turned me into a prodigal child. I was the one to put the taint on the Westbrook name."

"Did your parents say that? Or you—"

"I mean not outright, but the offhanded remarks here and there..."

I caressed her arms. "On the other hand, African parents are almost never underhanded. They say whatever they feel. No matter who they hurt."

Zola chuckled then looked on absently before continuing. "That position was held by my older sister prior. She's married to a white man, but at least she remained married. Since the band aid was off, I did something else insane like quit my job and pursue my passion."

"Dance."

She nodded. Earlier she told me the influence of Janet Wilson on her when she was a kid and then later, Misty Copeland. Her parents were supportive of her passion, buying everything she needed, paying for additional classes and entering her into competitions. However, they drew the line when it came to her making it a career.

"This time around, although I was so mad at you and I didn't have a choice, I wouldn't have wanted a big wedding."

"Baby, you always had a choice."

"Really? What if I had said no?"

"Then your dad would've had to explain to your mom why she gotta pack all her expensive stuff and move to an apartment."

"You're such a mess. So, that would have been it… with us?" She cocked her head to the side.

I turned her to fully face me. "Truthfully?"

"Of course."

I tucked her hair behind her ear. "That would have been it for *them*. You, on the other hand, If I had my way, I would've pulled out all the resources in my arsenal to pursue you until you caved."

"Smooth buddy."

"It's the truth."

"I didn't want all the fuss and now everyone seems so offended."

"They'll be all right. We gotta do this again when we go to Enugu in a few weeks. But at the end of the day, everyone is entitled to how they feel. We know what it is."

We sat for a few moments in palpable silence, taking in the melodic jazz playing in the background.

"You never talk about Uju's mom. What was she like?"

Taking a breath, I realized we hadn't talked about Eno and that was unfair. We'd talked about her ex, how they met, got married and how his controlling ways and temper led to their final demise. Although it was something I didn't like doing, I let out a sigh and gave my wife what she deserved.

My vulnerability.

"I was a year away from completing my program in South Africa when we found out we were expecting. We married a year out of college, and we'd done all the rites and the church wedding at home in Nigeria. She was finishing her own program in New York and was staying with her sister. The plan was for her to move back to Atlanta with me once I finished school, but that never happened."

Zola held me close as I recounted how I flew back and forth during Eno's pregnancy. "When she went into labor, I was by her side. Everything appeared all right; we welcomed our daughter Uju into the world. In a matter of minutes, though, alarms were blaring. Next thing I knew, I was being told she had some complications.

"The pain and grief of such an experience are overwhelming. To have been blessed with a child, then immediately have your world taken away – it seemed cruel to me. People tell you how to cope, but no one can understand the anguish of planning your life with someone, then having them gone so quickly. I could barely function – so I vowed never to go through something like that again."

"Baby, I'm so sorry. How did you manage with JuJu?"

"At first, I shut everyone out, determined to raise Uju myself. I think on some level, I was punishing myself for being here and Eno wasn't. The day I nearly burned the house down from exhaustion from dealing with a newborn, my cousins staged an intervention, and my mother was flown in."

For a moment we both sat in silence, lost in our thoughts. The light mood had given way to pregnant tension. Something I didn't want for us, but I had run away from the conversation long enough. I continued to caress Zola's arm until she slowly drifted off. Her gentle breathing was soothing in the quiet of the night.

I had to get her home. My feelings for my wife were deepening faster than expected. I promised my cousins I would be open to the possibility of love, especially for Uju. However, talking about Eno tonight reminded me of why I'd fought so hard to keep that door closed. No matter how hard I tried, my thoughts always came back to the fear of loss. I looked down at my wife who was snuggled up against me. I loved Eno, but this feeling I had for Zola was visceral. She'd shifted something in my soul. I wouldn't survive anything happening to her. If something did, where would that leave Uju?

I'd be out of town for a week. That should give me the space to take a step back and process what was happening. The price I'd paid for love was too steep, and it scared me to the point of insanity that I was opening myself to the risk again.

10

ZOLA

'Saiah: Zee, I know you don't think you're off the hook.

Jah: She chooses the time we are away to sneak her so-called husband to Luxe

Jeremy: I know those Kalu men, and they must be out of their minds. They would never go for the stuff they pulled.

Noah: Y'all give Zee a break. I met him. He wasn't so bad. Dad was pissed but mom is okay with the dude.

Zekia: I agree, she's grown. If this makes her happy…

'Saiah: Zee, I know you see us talking to you. If we pop up at your door, don't say we didn't try to talk to you first.

My sibling group chat had been blowing up since Monday morning. After answering the first couple of messages, I left the rest on read. Four days later and my brothers were still wound up. I had nothing else to add as I had bigger problems.

One was the future of Leap & Twirl. My eyes darted to the clock on my office wall. Mrs. Donovan would be here any minute to talk about my plans for the studio. I was leaning toward buying it, but there were some details I still wanted hashed out.

Two, and most important, was figuring out why the husband my brothers gave me so much grief about was acting funny. We had a great time in Luxe Noir. That was after his talk with my dad. I still had no idea what they discussed, but they were both strong-willed men, so I knew they didn't have a tea party. But after that, lunch was filled with a little less tension, and we had a great time.

Dinner that evening on the yacht was everything I dreamed of, but never got to experience with my first marriage. After making sure Ju and my mom were settled, I went to get ready. Feeling sexy, I dressed in an outfit I hadn't dreamed of wearing in a while. Flashbacks of my time with Caleb came roaring back. While we were dating, he'd give his opinion on what I'd wear, what I said when we were entertaining, about my career and most especially about my friendship with Tessa. He was controlling, but not overtly so, until we got married.

Magnify everything he did before along with being a tattle tale. There was nothing that happened in our home that my parents and his didn't know about within a few days. Truthfully, the fact that Jidenna didn't cave to my dad was a serious turn on.

When he arrived to pick me up for dinner, I half expected him to talk about my dress. It was tasteful, but showed a lot of skin. Apart from a few threats about gorging out other men's eyes if they stared for too long, he made me feel like a princess with the way he catered to me all night. The following day, he met Noah and Zuri. After church, we all went to brunch, then the men played a round of golf on the island resort while my mom, Zuri, Ju, and I sat for tea at the clubhouse. Before we left for

Atlanta, my mom had insisted we have a wedding reception very soon.

Since my husband was going out of town the following day. He, I and Uju spent a quiet evening at home. Jidenna was sandwiched between Uju and I while we watched *SING 2*, a movie I knew Uju had watched more times than I could count. While my little baby sang her heart out with the characters, my big baby was peppering kisses on my neck, temple, behind my ears along with discreet gentle caresses that drove me wild. His fingers brushed up against my lounge pants clad thighs, sending shivers up my spine.

Every time we were together, I could feel the electricity sparking between us, making my heart race and my breath catch in my throat. At some time during the night, without saying a word, he leaned in and kissed me deeply. His lips were soft and tasted like the mix of his drink and menthol from the mint he loved sucking on. I responded eagerly, caressing the side of his face until my moan made Uju turn to us.

"Eww, that is so gross."

I laughed, remembering the scowl on her face. After telling us how the koala from the movie didn't need to see that, she asked if she could go to her room. Later, I tucked her in, something I and her dad took turns doing. Then I went to help my husband pack while we talked. Our banter was light, and we both were good at teasing each other while we shared our schedules for the week. I spent a lot of time asking him about the Kalus and what to expect when we went to his home. Jasmine and Reign had filled me in a bit, but I wanted his point of view. Leave it to a man to tell me, "*Olaedo m*, everything will be fine. I'll make sure of it."

With the way he had been behaving these past four days, I wasn't sure anymore. I understood he was attending a conference. But these dry conversations and his eagerness to get off the phone to handle something he couldn't share with me were getting on my nerves. I understood we were still new, but if we had any chance of working, he needed to communicate. That was something he told me when I tried to hide my parents' reaction to our marriage from him.

> Zuri: So, you just gonna ignore your siblings?
> LOL

I looked down at my phone, smiling at my sister's text in our private thread. Picking up my Mango Dragon Fruit Starbucks Refresher, I took a sip before responding.

> Yep. I answered all of them at that impromptu group call we had a few days ago.

> Zuri: You know Isaiah and Elijah are not going to let up.

> Good thing my husband can hold his own.

> Zuri: I like it. It's giving that's my man and I'mma stick beside him.

Sending her a couple of laughing emojis at her reference, I shook my head.

> Zuri: What's Jeremiah's deal?

I rolled my eyes at the mention of my third oldest brother. He went on about meeting Cheta at some baseball charity event hosted by the team owner Darius Gray. According to my brother, Cheta was cocky and condescending. However, I knew my brother. He probably tried to show that he had money and Cheta, not one to back down, tried to show he had bigger money. Whatever the case, it had nothing to do with me. I told Zuri and she agreed with my assessment.

My chat with my sister was interrupted when there was a tap

on my door announcing Mrs. Donovan. The older woman in her late sixties made her appearance a few seconds later. The cheerful smile I was used to was in place as I ushered her to the couch in the corner of my office.

"I haven't been here in almost nine months, and I love that you took advantage of the autonomy I gave to you. The place looks spectacular," she said.

I had upgraded the HVAC, expanded the waiting area, sound-proofed more of the dance room and changed the flooring. Although she knew about what I wanted to do, she wanted no say in the decisions that came with it. According to my husband, I was doing the job of the owner while still doing work I was passionate about. Truth be told, Mrs. Donovan was my safety net. But Tessa and Jidenna were right, I was already doing everything an owner did without the title.

"Thank you. Let me get my laptop so we can discuss some of the details I have in mind before we finalize the sale."

"Sounds good."

I walked over to my desk and picked up my laptop. In five weeks, this was the second big decision I was making. I really didn't want to second guess myself like my husband was making me do with the first.

"When I brought my child to your school this morning, she was whole. So somebody better start explaining to me how she got a sprained wrist."

My hands shook and I could literally taste the anger in my mouth. My heart dropped to the bottom of my stomach when I got the call from Uju's school that she was injured and needed to be picked up. She had a wrist brace on now and the school nurse assured me she was okay. I was still taking her to the hospital, but not before I got answers from the principal.

"Mrs. Kalu, I can assure you that what happened here was a misunderstanding between a group of friends," Ms. Peters, the principal of the school, said.

"That girl is not my friend."

I turned and narrowed my eyes at Uju, sending her an unspoken warning. We had discussed speaking out of turn, especially when adults were talking.

"Sorry," she muttered.

Even before I married her father, Uju told me about the girls who suddenly found pleasure in teasing her. After the day she talked to me in my studio, we had frequent talks about everything she was curious about. Recently, we developed a routine of having girl talk. Either in the morning when she was getting ready for school or when we baked, and we loved doing it together.

I really did love that little girl, and somebody had to explain to me why the school administration knew of a problem, but allowed it to get to the point where my child was injured.

"Misunderstanding? Some girls my child was trying to ignore tripped her, she fell and then had to swing back, and you call that a misunderstanding? My husband has been here, and you *assured* him that this wouldn't happen again. I'm sure that nothing was done because if it was, those girls won't be so emboldened as to now trip my daughter. And because she defended herself, you have the nerve to talk of suspension?"

"Mrs. Kalu, please calm down. We do not condone hitting of any kind. I assure you that—"

"There goes that word again. You can't *assure* me of anything. But I can assure you of this, my daughter will be back at school on Monday. If she gets so much as a scratch or is treated any differently, I will tie this school district up in so much litigation that they won't know which way is up. You know who her father is; I suggest you research who I am."

I watched as the principal shifted uncomfortably in her seat. I didn't need her response as I had said all that needed to be said. I reached out to Uju who took my hand and we headed for the door. Next stop was the hospital then calling her dad. His big presentation was the next day, so it was going to take everything in me to convince him not to get on a flight tonight.

The next morning, I stood at the bottom of the stairs waiting on Uju. After talking to Jidenna last night, he agreed with me that Uju should stay home today. He'd be back later this evening. But instead of staying at home, Uju and I were having a well-deserved day of pampering starting with breakfast, a trip to the nail salon before ending our day with some retail therapy and lunch.

"JuJu, what's taking so long? Do you need help?"

When I went into her room a few minutes ago, Little Miss Independent explained that she was a big girl and could put on her clothes herself. Normally I didn't bother her, but because of her wrist, I wanted to help, but she insisted. A few seconds later, I watched as she scurried down the hallway on her way to the stairs.

"I'm ready."

I inspected the short-sleeved, black and pink graphic tee she wore over pink, flap pocket pants. With her braids still in the ponytail I put it in yesterday, she looked exactly like my husband's mini me. I'd seen a picture of her mother and all she did was carry Uju.

"You look beautiful. Where are your sunshades?"

"Thank you. You too. They're in my bag." She reached into her bag to show me the pink framed glasses.

Glancing down at my short-sleeved, two-piece brown and black print patchwork set, I smiled and replied, "Thank you, Ju. You ready?"

We entered the garage and since the weather was so nice, I opted for my husband's truck so we could let down the sunroof.

Before we left the property, Uju and I took a selfie and sent it to Jidenna.

On our way out. See you soon.

Hubby: You ladies look gorgeous. Have fun but not too much. See y'all tonight.

After wishing him good luck on his presentation, we headed to breakfast. Soon after, I started getting notifications on Instagram. When we got to the light, I picked up my phone to check out what was going on. The tag led me to Jidenna's page. He had the picture of Uju and I on his profile with the caption, *my world, my everything*. I put a heart emoji under the picture and went back to the GPS.

After we talked about Uju last night, he wasn't as distant as he had been the past couple of days. He was confusing me, and we needed to talk. I remembered Tessa telling me not to make this what it wasn't. Jidenna was all over me, so I needed clear clarification of what this was.

Several hours later, Uju and I were seated in a booth having lunch at a restaurant in Atlantic Station. After breakfast, we went to the nail salon and then I had to make an impromptu visit to the studio. We stayed there for a couple of hours before Uju and I headed to the mall. As we ate our burgers, she told me what she liked about her Enugu grandma and my mom.

Then suddenly, she paused. "I have never called anyone mummy before. Can I call you mummy, Ms. Zola?"

I was taken aback by the sudden change in subject, my heart pounding as Uju's big brown eyes met mine. I'd also never been called "mummy" before, and her request filled me with a warmth that spread through my entire body. Uju looked at me with wide, trusting eyes and I was struck with her innocence and vulnerability.

We hadn't discussed how to handle this situation, but Jidenna and I had agreed our primary goal was making the transition seamless for Uju. She fiddled nervously with her straw, searching my face for an answer. Unsure of what to say, I threw it back to her.

"You can call me whatever you feel comfortable with, sweetie," I murmured softly.

Uju placed her index finger over her lips thoughtfully before replying, "Okay, since you and my daddy said my mummy was watching me from heaven, while you will watch me here...how about if I call you Mummy Zola?"

A single tear rolled down my cheek as I nodded mutely, overcome with too much emotion to even speak. Uju threw her arms around me tightly and I laughed through my tears, feeling a surge of hope rush through me. As our embrace lingered on, I thought of the future that could be ours, but knew I had to get my husband on the same page first.

Later that night, I watched as Jidenna ate his dinner at the kitchen island. After lunch with Uju, we went back to the studio in time for me to teach her dance class. Instead of staying to lock up, I got Anna to do it. Uju tired herself out from the activities of the day, so it was easy to get her to take a shower and head to bed. Right before my shower, Jidenna texted me that his plane had landed. I heated up the food we got for him and placed it in the warmer.

"Speak baby, you're making me nervous."

He looked up from his plate. I had been hovering under the guise of cleaning up the kitchen. I didn't cook so I was sure he knew it was a rouse, but I didn't know how to ask him what had been running through my mind all week. Partly because I feared his answer.

"Are we okay?"

He frowned at me mid bite. "Whatchu mean?"

"We were good when we left Luxe, but I sensed a shift when you were in Chicago. Is everything okay?"

"We're good, baby."

Annoyed with his nonchalance, my anger surged. "You're going to have to give me more than that. Those dry answers you gave me, me having to ask you a million times before you answered one question, and you always having to get off the phone because something came up… All of a sudden, you're moving real funny and I need to know why."

Jidenna stared at me for a few minutes before standing to empty the remnants of his food. I fumed as I watched him take his plate to the sink, when he turned on the faucet to wash his plate, I lost it.

"Look, if you need time to think about this again, I can go home, and you —"

Before I could understand what was happening, Jidenna was on me, encasing me between the granite countertop and his body.

"Are you out of your mind? What home? This is the only home you have. Here…with me! I am your home, and you are mine. Just moments ago, you told me about what you did in the principal's office at my daughter's school, then her asking to call you mummy with a plea not to leave her…again, and you turn around and talk about going home?" His voice was harsher than I thought it needed to be.

"I wasn't talking about her! I was talking about you." Failing at my attempt to push him back, my chest burned with frustration.

"Guess what? We're a package deal. I was searching for the right words to apologize because your feelings are valid. But you wanna talk of leaving before we've even begun?" His voice rose with intensity. "If *home* is that condo you got, we're about to sell that joint or put it up for lease. This is your home, Zola Kalu."

"Then you better start learning how to communicate instead of shutting me out."

"Nobody is shutting you out, but can I process, please! Can you allow me that?"

"Then communicate that!" I wasn't backing down from this. He could be mad all he wanted, but I had spent the majority of my first marriage ignoring things until I suffocated. This would not be that.

Jidenna invaded my space, the heat of his body scorching me. His hand curled around my bottom as he yanked me to him, pressing me so tightly against him that I could barely breathe. His lips hovered over mine. His breath like fire on my skin. "We don't run. Ever. You don't even think of it. Do you understand me?"

Like he knew it would, my body betrayed me, and I melted into him. His cologne smelled of musk, sandalwood, and something spicy almost sending me off a cliff, but I struggled to maintain my train of thought. "Why...why...what was the attitude change about?"

Ignoring me, he demanded in a harsh whisper. "Answer me. Do you understand?"

"Ye...yes," I croaked out.

There was a long dangling pause before he spoke again. This time in a subdued tone. "The realization that I was falling in love with you hit me in the chest and the clamp of fear had my heart in a vice. I can't think or breathe properly when you're in the room. You consume me whole and for a minute, my thoughts went to what I'll do if anything happened to you."

My mind blanked at his confession. "Nothing is going to happen to me," I whispered, my throat clogged with emotion.

Jidenna's dark eyes locked onto mine, sparks jumping between us. His hands moved around my waist and pulled me closer to him until I felt our hearts hammering in unison. I grabbed the back of his shirt and tugged it off quickly. His hands moved up my body, exploring every inch until I gasped with pleasure. He captured my lips in a fiery kiss and with a suddenness that sent shivers across my skin, he lifted me. My legs went instinctively around his waist as we made our way to the stairs.

With my head cradled against his chest, he entered the room

and stumbled forward, and we fell together onto the bed. Our bodies intertwined in a wildfire of passion. Tremors of delight traveled along my spine as his lips pressed hard against my neck. Jidenna's body was like a masterpiece, and I savored the feeling of his muscles under my fingertips. We indulged in each other frantically, spending the next several minutes finally consummating our marriage. When our passion reached its peak, we shouted out each other's names in ecstasy until we were lost in a blissful haze.

After a shower, we both slipped into bed together. I could feel my husband's chest rise and fall with every breath as I nestled my head against him. The thought of how this would affect our relationship filled me with contentment, and before long I had fallen into a deep sleep.

11

———

JIDENNA

"*E*meka, the math is not mathing. I hope for the sake of you and your future children, you're not spending our money on these chewing gum girls. Especially since you got a wife."

As Cheta roared, almost breathing down the man's throat, I sat with my leg crossed over my knee. I was sure he was inhaling that man's breath with how close he was, yelling at him. It didn't take all that talking to get the message across, but I let my cousin do him. He was always going to anyway.

With my cap covering my eyes, I turned to Arinze. He knew I was asking him to intervene, but he ignored me. I could understand their anger. I was equally as furious because this man had lied to my face so many times. But I didn't have time to go upside his head today. I needed to get home to my wife before my grandmother and mother questioned her to death. Zola was in safe hands since my sister was there, but nobody could protect her like me, so we needed to wrap this up.

I stood and walked over to Emeka, who was our manager at Tune Up in Enugu. The salon had state-of-the-art equipment for men to enjoy a day of self-care, grooming and pampering. Not to

119

diminish what women went through, but men often had a lot on their shoulders that they couldn't share for the sake of being looked at as weak or soft. They also needed pampering and self-care.

Tune Up was several steps up from a regular barber shop. With a sauna, manicure and pedicure, facial treatment station, barber area and meditation room, we had it all. There was no doubt in my mind that we were making money. The issue was, lately the money wasn't coming in the way it used to, but the logs showed that our customers had increased. I could tell by all the tags I got on social media.

Moving Cheta to the side, I leaned forward. "Emeka, you know me."

He nodded.

"Good. You remember what I can do."

Again, he nodded. In high school, one of his cousins thought it was a wise idea to mess with my older sister. Before Arinze and Cheta had an idea of what was going on, I had broken the dude's jaw and hand. I wasn't proud of some of the things I had done, however I had done them.

"So, this is how this will go down. We'll be around for two weeks. That's the amount of time you have to make this right. *I na-anụ ihe m na-agwa gị?*"

"*Anụla m,*" he said, confirming his understanding of what I had told him.

I stood straight and motioned to my cousins for us to head out. It was late-June. My family and I had arrived in Enugu four days ago. I followed Arinze and Cheta's lead and gave my wife some time to settle in before leaving her with the family. Zola's case was different though. Unlike Jasmine and Reign, who popped up as a surprise, Zola and my mother communicated over the phone right after we got married. She had also spoken to my dad and sisters.

After they were initially welcomed by my family, I asked that

Zola and Uju be given time to rest. Uju claimed she didn't need to, and Zola thought it would make her look bougie if she stayed away.

"Look bougie? Baby, you *are* bougie. You arrange all our towels by a specific color palette, you must have an iced matcha latte every day from Starbucks, and might I remind you that we had to buy cartons of Flow water for the trip over here," I had explained to my wife earlier. Laughing, she called me a hater before walking out of our room to go to Uju's.

"This guy, you and all your mafia moves," Arinze teased once we were out of the office.

"Are you minding him? Drizzle thinking he's Steven Segal," Cheta said.

"Have you forgotten I am both those things? It got the job done, didn't it?"

For a period in college, I was part of a group that served as vigilantes on campus. I went by the name Drizzle, because people said it was gonna be a gloomy day when I appeared on the scene.

One semester, there had been an uptick in crime and assault against women. So a group of us got licensed to carry. With approval from the school, we got trained and patrolled the campus. That was how I met Eno. Her friend had been harmed when her purse was snatched from her. Everything was going well until one of the vigilantes forgot his limitations and beat someone unconscious, causing the school to revoke our authorization pending an investigation. I left the group after that.

My cousins and I continued to tease each other until we got to the lobby. The front of the salon was quiet, with only a few customers waiting for their appointments. I smiled at them, trying to convey a sense of professionalism and gratitude. As we made a right towards the VIP section of the salon, I heard commotion coming from the area. Hurrying over, we saw one of the barbers was dealing with a customer who had his hands folded across his chest.

"What do you mean, you don't know how to cut a Caesar with the curly top? Isn't that your job?"

On further inspection, he looked familiar. I looked at Cheta for confirmation and he nodded. I didn't have time for this headache today. But if one of us didn't intervene, Kamal Danjuma would tear up this shop and gladly pay for the damages later.

"*Oga, no vex*. Can you please show me a picture of what you're looking for?" the barber asked.

"Big bros, *ke kwanu?*" Cheta greeted Kamal.

Kamal looked over at all three of us before replacing his scowl with a smile. He shook each one of us before introducing his son and nephews to us. None of us knew the Danjumas personally, but their mother was from Enugu. Many years ago, news broke that their mother married a northerner who abandoned her and their three boys in London then moved to Nigeria to be with his second wife.

Kamal, a retired internationally known soccer player, was the youngest of the brothers. Cheta met him when he was wrapping up his final season of play in America before he moved to London to play for a club there and finish out his career. If people thought my cousin was bad, they hadn't met Kamal Danjuma. It's no wonder Cheta looked up to the guy.

"What are you doing in town?" Arinze asked.

"My mother is being given one church title." He waved its importance off, then continued, "I don't know what it's called, but when she or the wife say show up, I'm there." He glanced over at his son and nephews who were engrossed with a game on a phone.

"How are you guys hiring people who don't know how to do a Caesar?" Kamal asked.

By now, Emeka had joined us and pulled the barber to the side, showing him something on his phone. I hoped it was the picture. Kamal was the big homie, and no one survived on his bad side. He wasn't on social media a lot, but his jabs were lethal for anyone who crossed him.

"Don't worry, we'll take care of it," I said, going over and instructing Emeka to send another barber in.

"It's a good thing he said he didn't know how to do it before he messed up my son's head. Because..." he narrowed his eyes at Cheta who chuckled.

I'm glad too.

Minutes later, after some more small talk and ensuring the new barber knew what he was doing, we made our way to the door. Then Cheta turned, "We've been hearing some chatter in the street about you and a certain league."

Kamal shrugged. "It's gonna remain in the streets until it comes from me."

Laughing, we made our way to the exit. I was sure that all the customers were satisfied. Now, it was time to head home to my family.

~

"Wow Daddy, you look great!" Uju circled me, examining every detail of my appearance.

"Thanks, Ju." I spun the platinum and gold band on my ring finger, laughing at her enthusiasm.

After spending time with my cousins, I took Uju and Zola to Unity Park. The park was doing a good job of living up to the reason it was created, which was to recreate some of the history torn down by the city's need for urbanization. The huge, roaring lion sculpture, indoor entertainment and a water pond deep enough for boat riding were among the attractions my girls loved. Now, it was time for some alone time with my wife.

"Okay Daddy, Mummy Zola's outfit is better than yours." Uju's assessment had me turning my head to the stairs.

Zola glided down in a floral print, long-sleeved dress that was belted at the waist and stopped above her knees. I wasn't sure what material it was, but it moved around her like it was very light. On her manicured feet were orange heeled sandals which highlighted her pink toenails and matched her clutch. My wife was so girly, and I found that so attractive. Her colors complemented the orange and black traditional print set I had on.

"Thank you, my JuJu." Zola twirled and kissed Uju on her forehead. "Make sure you do what Auntie Onyi tells you."

Mesmerized by her presence, I walked up to Zola and snaked my arm around her waist and pulled her closer. I nuzzled her neck and laughed when I heard Uju groan. Soon after, my sister arrived. After handing Uju off to her, I escorted Zola to my truck for our night on the town.

Forty-five minutes later, with one hand on the steering wheel and the other rested on its new favorite place – my wife's thighs – I brought my car to a stop in the valet section of the Sip 'n Paint studio where we were starting off the night.

"I've never done this before," she said.

Her excitement elicited a wink from me before I exited the car. As I gave the valet my keys, my eyes caught a second attendant trying to open the door for Zola. After hollering over to him that I got it, I walked around and opened her door. She learned quick just as Uju did that they didn't open doors for themselves when I was around. Zola stepped out of the car, and I kissed her temple before grabbing her hand to lead her inside.

"Roller Coaster" by Burna Boy ft. J Blavin floated through the air as we entered the studio. The space was well lit with colorful artwork on the walls and a snack table in the corner. We were greeted by the instructor who ushered us to our seats at the back of the room. Since my arthouse wasn't too far from here and I was a Kalu, I expected to be recognized, but luckily those who did, accepted the head nod I gave and stayed put.

What really had their attention though was my wife. I knew for a fact, she was the finest woman in the world, but my biggest source of pride was that she was mine. I was good as long as their eyes didn't linger, and no one touched. I'd hate a repeat of what happened the day before.

My cousins and I had taken our women out to eat at one eatery Jasmine couldn't stop talking about. She wanted to try the place out again since she loved their food the first time she visited. We all know that anything Jasmine wanted, Arinze provided.

Although my cousins were both internationally known, I visited home more than they did and I worked a lot with local talent, so folks recognized me as much as they did them. A fan kept trying to get my attention, hollering out questions. I was kind enough to tell him that I was with my family, and I'd answer his question on our way out. I guess he thought I needed to be on his time because he had the audacity to touch my wife, asking her to "beg" me. The sight of his hands on her arm caused rage to surge through me. Most Nigerians had a touching problem, but after yesterday, his bloody nose would always be a reminder that people should never touch what was mine.

The instructor set up our canvases, wooden easels, paintbrushes, and paint. I pulled Zola's stool out from under the table and stepped back.

"Aren't you going to be bored, considering you're an artist?"

"Art is always interesting to me, but I'll admit that painting isn't my strong suit."

"So, I have a chance of creating a masterpiece while you come up with nonsense?" She let out a small chuckle and eased herself into her seat.

"It's an instructional class, baby. I doubt I'll be that bad. But go ahead Zola Picasso, let's see what you got."

She moved her shoulders, dancing in place to the beat of the music. Satisfaction at her joy flooded over me as I softly caressed the nape of her neck. She leaned her head back against my abdomen and puckered her lips. I pressed mine briefly against hers before taking my seat beside her. We gave the instructor our attention as the class began.

Later that night, Zola perched herself on top the truck's hood in front of our home. Her legs were spread apart just enough for me to stand between them. With my arms around her waist, I rested my head on her chest. I felt the warmth of her fingertips as they ran gently up and down my back. It was almost midnight and neither of us were ready to go inside.

After the painting class, we went to a restaurant that recently opened in the heart of the city. The service was fantastic, and the ambiance set the mood for a romantic dinner. They served different kinds of cuisines, but Zola was feeling a bit adventurous and didn't opt for the familiar. I liked her willingness to learn the culture and eagerness to assimilate to it, but I wasn't allowing her do anything that might upset her stomach. After a dinner of spicy native rice and cow leg with a few mocktails, we strolled hand in hand along a scenic path to walk some of it off.

On our way, we met a group of *atilogwu* dancers practicing choreography in the open field. I could feel the excitement vibrating off my wife, so we went closer. After following their movements which included synchronized vigorous body movements and some acrobatics for several minutes, Zola asked me if they would be upset if she joined them. In our native language, I asked them to teach her a few moves, offering to contribute to their troupe. For the next half hour, with her shoes in my hand, I watched with contentment as Zola danced with no care in the world. She seemed light and I was happy.

We were two people given a second chance at love, and I tried to remember that and be grateful any time fear crept up my spine. I wasn't afraid to admit that the thought paralyzed me most days. It had been weeks since our argument and I was happy with the way things were.

My wife wanted to dig into feelings that I wanted to forget. She often cited that she shared about her divorce, but as selfish as it sounded, her letting go of a man who was doing her wrong was very different from a woman I loved being snatched away from me by death.

"You ready for the day after tomorrow?" Zola asked, breaking the palpable silence we'd been relishing in.

The big celebration was in two days and after that, we'd leave Uju in Enugu to fly back to the US with my cousins while my wife and I headed to Abuja. The meeting with the marketing director for Zeidu Fashions would take place there. Once that was done, we'd fly out to enjoy the surprise I had set up for my wife. Several days of blissful solitude by the ocean, just the two of us.

"What's there to get ready for? Attend the special church service then dance the night away?"

"Four decades with the same person? Man, I wonder how your parents or even mine for that matter made it that long."

"Well, you need to ask them because I expect for you to be able to talk from experience when our daughter asks you the same question."

She lifted my face from her bosom. "You do know that I didn't marry myself."

I scoffed and resumed my position. "Of course, I do. I'm setting the expectation because I'm already on board."

"And what exactly are you on board with?"

This time I lifted my head and stood to my full height. I wanted her to hear me clearly. God gave me a way to make her, the woman that had entrenched herself into my soul, mine sooner than I expected without the usual expectations and struggles. Still, I was determined not to let her think our marriage didn't stand the chance of longevity.

Since we'd been married, I couldn't deny the truth. Although ghosting her wasn't the best way to go about it, I was right when I told her I was avoiding what I knew I'd become with her. Obsessed. I could admit I'd gone from lust to a passionate craving deeper than anything I have ever felt before.

I tightened my arms around her waist, enjoying the intimacy of our connection. "I am on board with my commitment to being your partner and serving you the best I can. I intend to support your dreams, work on better communication, and build a great future together. You have my love, respect, and loyalty."

My gaze held her eyes. "I know in theory, all these things sound nice and since I'm human, I know that my intent might not always come across as it should, so I promise to be teachable and seek the guidance from Jireh so I can be the husband that you need, want, and deserve."

A single tear escaped down her cheek, so I gently brushed it away with my thumb. Sometimes my wife was such a crybaby. I smiled. "*Olaedo m*, you're making my chest tight with those tears. Stop it."

She narrowed her eyes at me and sniffed. "I can't help it. You can be so closed off sometimes, so when you say such things..." She closed her eyes and sniffed again. Reopening them, she continued. "...but I promise not to take your vulnerability for granted. I've been in love with you for a long time. How or when, I can't tell you. When you disappeared on me, I was angry because you took a piece of me, I didn't think you deserved, and I wanted it back. I have no idea what the future holds, but I'm committed to loving you in all your forms."

"I got something for you." Opening the car door, I retrieved a velvet box from the glove compartment and handed it to her.

"What's this?" she asked, opening the case. Her eyes lit up, glancing at me briefly before returning her attention to the piece.

A quick study of my wife's jewelry box told me she didn't wear gold. Inside the box was a beautiful silver necklace with her birthstone set in the middle of the letter "O" with a silver under-lay. I'd spent weeks designing the perfect necklace I wanted to always see on her neck. The box also contained an antique locket made of polished silver with a series of intricate repeating, "J" the infinity symbol and "Z" carved into the metal in an ancient script. Inside the locket was the inscription, *Today, Tomorrow, Always.*

"They're both so beautiful. Thank you, baby," she whispered, her eyes shining with emotion.

I leaned in and kissed her softly, savoring the feel of her lips against mine. This was the woman who complemented me in every way possible. Together, we would face whatever challenges came our way, and we would emerge victorious. As our lips parted, I gazed into her eyes and relished the tenderness of her smile. I knew that I would strive to always keep it in place.

"You're welcome, baby. Which one do you want me to put on?"

Zola handed me the necklace with her birthstone. She asked me if it stood for my pet name for her to which I nodded. After getting it on, I kissed her neck.

"I'm going to save this one so I can put our kids picture on the other side of the locket."

My heart froze in my chest. Children? She wanted children? Now that I thought about it, we'd never discussed it. She never brought it up and so I let it be. The child I loved with my whole heart had cost me the woman I loved. Was that a tradeoff I was willing to make again? Her eyes were fixed on the locket, and I could see the joy and hope in them. A wave of guilt collapsed into me as I thought of betraying that hope. She deserved everything she desired.

I forced a smile as my heart pounded fiercely in my chest and sweat clammed my palms. The fear of loss fought within me with the desire for her happiness. It was a torturous dilemma I had to face. I silently prayed that when the time came, her joy would win the day.

12

ZOLA

I was in love with this kitchen. It was bright and white, a stark contrast to the dark mahogany of the cabinets. The all stainless-steel appliances looked sleeker on the slab of white marble that was used for the countertops. In fact, I adored everything about this house. Jasmine and Reign tried to give me a heads up, but I couldn't put my head around it.

With my parents, I had visited Egypt, South Africa, and Senegal, but never Nigeria. I hadn't even heard of Enugu until Jidenna told me that was where he was from. The day after we arrived, Uju and her dad took me on a tour of the house. The six-bedroom, five-bath home was fully equipped with a media room, man cave, game room, an art studio for Jidenna and what absolutely broke me was when he showed me a brand-new dance room. I could tell it was a new addition. I didn't understand why as I wasn't sure how often we would be visiting Enugu.

Wiping the tear at the corner of my eye, he answered. "My wife's presence will always be known in any space I occupy."

At the back of the house, I could tell he spared no expense for Uju. She had a huge walk-in doll house and her own bouncing castle. There was also a gated pool and a huge deck. The house wasn't the only thing that was fascinating, the town itself was. If I wasn't being escorted around town by my parents-in-law, then a driver and security would drive me, Jasmine, and Reign around to places they had been.

The day we left without security, even though Arinze's sister and Jidenna's sister were with us, Arinze lost his mind when we returned. I understood that Jasmine was pregnant, but I had never seen him so out of character. My husband, however, was upset for a different reason. Let him tell it, everyone was hoarding his wife. Dragging me to the house, he murmured something about how he should have followed Cheta's lead and kept everyone out of his house until he was ready. In all the commotion, Cheta and Reign just laughed and headed towards their home.

I was happy that Reign's relationship with her mother-in-law was better. Even Cheta's sisters tried to make amends during family dinner a few days ago, but Cheta was still suspicious. I was thrilled, however, that as much as my mom liked my husband, his mother liked me. Even their grandparents took to me. Their grandfather was frail, but he was still insistent on strolling around the compound with Jas, Rei and I most evenings.

"Mummy Zola, are you okay?"

Uju entering the kitchen brought me out of my reverie. I'm sure the chef thought I had lost my mind, staring off into space. I'd asked her to show me how to make the yam porridge my husband loved. The cubed white yams were boiling, but I still should've been paying attention.

In about three hours, the whole family would be headed to church for the Thanksgiving service for Jidenna's parents. Afterwards, we would celebrate at a venue in the heart of the city. I'd gone there yesterday with Jidenna's mom and sister and the place was simply amazing.

"I'm fine, Ju. Is your daddy back?"

"No, but he texted me and said he has been trying to reach you."

"Shoot." I went in search of my phone. I had left it in the living room when I brought down our clothes. The professional makeup and head tie ladies were in my parents-in-law's house, and that was where we would be getting ready. We were first up on the schedule before they moved to Reign's house.

My phone had three missed calls and a couple of text messages. I glanced at the ones from the group chat I had with Jas and Rei. After responding that we would be on time, I called my husband. He answered on the first ring.

"Woman, where have you been?"

"Hello to you too, my love."

"Stop playing with me. I was worried."

I rolled my eyes. His overprotectiveness wasn't new, but since the Sip 'n' Paint night two days ago, he'd been a little extra.

"Babe, you have security outside, and the compound entrance has armed guards. What can possibly happen to us?"

He sighed. "Just answer the phone when I call, please."

I acquiesced. His cousins had come to get him early in the morning. They had to handle something at Kalu International Inc., then head to Tune Up to get a touch up from their barber. After ensuring Uju and I were fine and running through our schedule, he told me he'd be running late and asked if I could put out his outfit.

"Mummy Zola, I was thinking about the theme for my party," Uju said, as she hopped onto the kitchen island.

I set the plate before her as she began telling me about Princess Tiana from the Disney movie. She looked at the food and smiled. After thanking me, she bowed her head and said grace. Although I didn't cook it exclusively by myself, I did a large percentage of the work and was proud of how my first Nigerian dish turned out. I wasn't a stranger to having domestic help, but I was the one out of all my siblings that loved to help them or my mother in the kitchen.

I sat beside Uju with my plate as she rattled off her ideas for her birthday party coming up in four months. When I first moved into Jidenna's home, I didn't know how this thing with Uju and I would work. Being her dance teacher and mothering her were two different things. What a difference three months made. Her daddy was even fake jealous of our relationship. Either he teased Uju to leave his wife alone or he would tease me to stop hoarding his daughter. The day Uju told him that his wife was her mummy, I nearly fell out laughing. My husband was big hurt. Before he would let it go, Uju and I had to bake him our special blueberry muffins. The man was so spoiled.

"I got your slippers out the car."

I leaned back into my husband. He knew exactly what I needed. With my head tie gone and my feet on fire, I was sure I looked a mess. My eyes roamed the reception hall, and the place was still lively, and most of the guests showed no signs of wanting to leave.

"Thank you." I turned to face him, and he got down on one knee and unbuckled my heels.

Sinking my feet into the slippers Reign insisted I brought with me, I sighed. Hours earlier, when we left the Kalu compound for church, I was dressed to the nines, and I loved it. I had a few African print sets I'd ordered from Amazon, but nothing could compare to wearing the real thing made here in Nigeria. The stylist had given me a light face beat just the way I described it to her and the head wrap woman had me looking like a true African princess.

Jidenna, his sisters, I and Uju wore the same fabric, while all the other members of the Kalu clan wore a similar, but slightly different fabric. The colors of the day were silver and magenta and again, Jasmine and Reign were right on the money. These people could party. What got me though was that as wealthy as the Kalus were, when his parents were doing their first dance, guests were spraying money on them with these money gun things. Even people who I'm sure didn't have the amount of money they had, were giving them money.

Jidenna explained to me that no matter one's status, they didn't show up to parties without money for spraying. It was rude. How much they sprayed was up to them, but the celebrants were not in the habit of policing anybody's pockets. Also, most of these people might want favors in the future and this was a way of making sure that they were seen.

"You good?" Jidenna rose to his full height, his face taut with exhaustion.

"Yeah, what about you? You've been running around all day."

He snaked his arm around my waist. "Yes, I'm good. My wife made sure I had something to eat."

I smiled, replying, "She sounds like a keeper."

His gaze softened and he leaned toward my ear. "Yeah, and I'm never letting her go."

I laughed and he brushed his lips against my temple. We swayed together to the melodic beat of one of the calmer Afrobeat songs I've heard. For a few moments, we were lost in each other, until Jidenna's mother tapped his shoulder.

She beamed at us before her eyes settled on my husband. "Nna, your father needs you. I want to talk to my daughter."

His brow furrowed and his eyes darted from her to me as if searching for answers I knew for sure I didn't have.

"Go. You must have me confused with your Aunty Amaka," his mother said.

I pressed my lips together to stifle my laughter. Aunty Amaka was Cheta's mom. The running joke in the family was that Cheta was scared to leave Reign alone with his mom. Something to do with her not being very receptive to Reign when she visited Enugu for the first time. I liked Cheta's mom, but everyone seemed to get their jabs in. I knew the wives all had a special connection. Anytime I was around them, it was evident. One wouldn't know they weren't sisters by blood. Jasmine, Reign, and I admired their bond and talked about working, despite our varying schedules to ensure we emulated them. So far, they were easy to get along with, so I didn't anticipate that being a problem.

Jidenna gave her a warning look and told me he would be back. Church was great, the reception was even better, but I was ready to call it a night. My mother-in-law pulled me to the side. The woman was gorgeous, very soft spoken and the little time I had spent with her and her husband, I knew the man bent to her will. It was beautiful to see. She had the power but didn't abuse it. Once we were alone, she looked at me with a small smile on her lips.

"*Nne m*, I just wanted to tell you how happy I am to have you as my new daughter," she said, her voice was soft, mirroring the look in her eyes.

I smiled, feeling grateful for her kind words. "Thank you so much, Mama. I'm blessed to be an addition to the family."

She nodded, her eyes still fixed on mine as she took my hands in hers. "My son has always been quiet, calculated and planned everything he does. A dark cloud has hung over him for years and since he isn't so expressive, I've been worried. But with you, he's different and every day, I put my knees on the ground and give God praise that he can smile again. *Daalu Nne*, thank you. With you, he seems to have found his anchor."

I wasn't sure how to respond to that, so I just smiled back at her.

She continued. "I also want to thank you for what you have done with my granddaughter. She is a totally different person from the one I saw some months ago." She let out a deep sigh. "Although everything was so quick and you and your husband robbed me of tying my *ichafu* high in the sky and dancing. I understand it was what both of you wanted."

I felt a sense of warmth spread through me. "Yes, it was. I love them both."

"Ha! You don't have to tell me. Everyone can see it." We shared a laugh. "It's one thing to talk on the phone, but to see it, my heart is overjoyed. However, my daughter, just like I told your husband earlier, I'm telling you, marriage is work. How hard or easy depends on both of you. My pastor said something in his sermon a long while ago that sticks with me to this day. I told my daughters and now I'm telling you.

"Mathew 13:44 speaks of a man who bought a treasure then buried it in an open field, then bought the entire field. Now, the treasure was secured, but he also owned all the unknown things in that field. Nice smelling flowers, weeds, snakes, a lovely pond...in other words, the good and bad aspects of the field. What I'm saying is that the road won't be easy, but remember why you started on the journey. That will keep you comforted when it gets rocky. Hold yourself to a high standard, but don't forget what drew both of you together."

"Thank you, Mama," I said, feeling a lump form in my throat. Although Jidenna kept assuring me his mother, who was a retired banker, was the most welcoming person I'd meet, I was still skeptical. She was his mother after all. But her genuineness was so refreshing that I was speechless. She drew me in for a hug. The warm embrace was a "welcome to the family" and "I love you" rolled into one and I relished it.

The wonders of God's creation.

The past couple of mornings, I'd woken up and walked just a few steps out to the Indian ocean from our beachside cottage. As I strolled down the coastline, my toes tingled with delight as the soft, white sand massaged them. The tranquil sound of the rolling waves crashing against the rocky shore enveloped me with a lightness I'd become familiar with in the past couple of months. Wrapping my light cardigan around me, I took a seat on a large boulder and drank in the breathtaking view before me. The azure crystal clear waters, peculiar rock formations, and the lush mountain in the distance. Capturing these images up close would cause one to know that the pictures on Instagram of Seychelles island and the experience of seeing the island up close couldn't be compared.

I couldn't begin to put into words the emotions that had overwhelmed me these past couple of days. Two days after the party, my husband and I kissed our baby girl goodbye and hopped on a plane to Abuja, Nigeria's capital. Although I didn't visit Lagos, Jidenna compared it to New York. But Abuja wasn't that way. It was calmer, but one could still tell it was the seat of the government.

The day we arrived, we got some food, checked on Uju and passed out from exhaustion. The next morning, we had breakfast on the balcony of our hotel after which Jidenna went for his meeting. He showed me the designs of the jewelry line and my man was so talented. I cried when he told me that he renamed the line, *ZoJu*, after his girls.

While he was out, I called my parents back in the US, texted Tessa, and took some pictures for the 'Gram before taking a nap. By the time he got back, we went out to dinner, saw some of the town, but then retired early to rest for my surprise trip the following day.

After so many hours on the private plane, I was annoyed that he wasn't telling me where we were going. My attitude didn't seem to faze him, so like a petulant child, I went to the back of the plane. It seemed I had only closed my eyes for a minute when Jidenna was nudging me to get up.

The first thing I noticed about Seychelles, the smallest

country in Africa which was actually a group of smaller islands, was that it was Black people deficient. Most of the people were either white or mixed race. Something that was immediately evident was their bias. I was shocked at how the immigration officials conveniently ushered the Black folks to the side. We joked about my husband and his Nigerian ego all the time. This time I wished he would let it go. He didn't.

After he raised the roof, we cleared customs and were given an escort to take us to our resort on Félicité Island. Upon entering Six Senses Resort, my jaw dropped at its sheer beauty. Our guest experience maker rattled off all the things we could do during our stay, but I was too mesmerized to listen. A private infinity pool overlooked the ocean while luxurious amenities such as a huge deck with sunbeds, a dining table, a humongous bed tented with a mosquito net, a bathtub, rain shower, and a flat-screen television with satellite channels awaited us in our suite—the perfect blend of paradise and opulence.

Feeling his presence, I turned, smiling when I saw my husband strolling toward me. His sexy gait had my head in a tizzy as I took him in. He was shirtless, displaying his well-toned abs. His knee length shorts hung low and matched his bucket hat. Although his eyes were covered with a pair of dark shades, I could feel his gaze on me. Reaching me, he pulled me up from the boulder and took my place before resting me comfortably on his lap. He peppered light kisses along my neck before inhaling my scent.

"Why didn't you wake me?"

"You were sleeping so peacefully. It would have been a crime. Besides you needed the rest. You've been going nonstop for weeks."

"I appreciate that." Squeezing me, we sat in comfortable silence for a few minutes, taking in the beauty around us. Finally, he spoke, "This is your honeymoon, baby. The next several days are all about you. Whatchu wanna do?"

"Well, the experience guy said—"

"When did you talk to him?"

I laughed. "Calm down. I called the main lobby." I shrugged. "Besides, he's not my type."

"Oh yeah? What's your type?"

"Grumpy, sarcastic, can hold a grudge, very handsome, loving, caring, attentive to detail, overprotective, confident but border-line arrogant, sexy Black king."

He leaned his head back and laughed. "I love you too, baby." Tapping my leg, I stood, and he followed suit. He grabbed my hand, and we began strolling back to our villa.

"It's still early. Let's see what we can get into today."

Days later, I listened to the sound of the waves crashing on the shore, and a cool breeze gently blowing through the curtains. Soft melodic sounds from the satellite station floated through the villa. Tomorrow was our last day on the island, and I'd never forget the experience. Our mornings normally started out the same, checking in on our daughter, then idling on the deck while eating a light breakfast. After showering together, which always set us back on time, we would get dressed and head out for a day of exploration.

We hopped on a boat and went island hopping, stopping at several of the neighboring islands to explore the local markets and soak up the sun on secluded beaches. We even saw some amazing wildlife, like giant tortoises and colorful birds. We also went hiking in the lush rainforest and saw some breathtaking waterfalls.

One day while we were on Mahe, the major island and seat of the government, we got to see what the locals called the Creole festival. It was basically a mixture of the various cultures on the island getting together to celebrate the unique makeup of the people.

In the evenings, we enjoyed a private dinner on the deck of our villa or in a secluded area of the restaurant in the main lobby.

My favorite was our beach dinners with the two of us, the sound of the ocean, and a saxophonist serenading us with soulful melodies for company. It was so romantic, as we talked, stole kisses, and savored every moment of the delicious meal. Sometimes the meal was local, at other times, we had a continental spread. Afterwards, we'd take long walks along the beach, hand in hand, discussing anything, everything, to nothing at all.

Earlier today, we decided to go snorkeling. I had to beg my husband to go with me. He absolutely refused to go under the water as he called it. Despite my pleas and sales pitch, he stayed on the boat. But made sure to threaten the tour guide with destruction if any harm came to me. He was so extra. When I got in, it was like swimming in an aquarium, with so many colorful fish and corals to see.

"*Ola m*…you want green or red grapes?" Jidenna yelled from the kitchen.

"Both."

"Greedy."

"Yeah, whatever. You love it."

We'd gone into the market earlier and bought fruits, cheeses, and a bottle of wine. Tonight, we wanted to do without the private chef or guest help. Jidenna was preparing a charcuterie board which we intended to enjoy while watching the sunset. It was the perfect way to end a day that was almost ruined by an overzealous tour guide and a husband who was short tempered. The couple's massage we had earlier helped melt the tension while Jidenna calmed down.

Minutes later, Jidenna set the tray down with our glasses. Then he returned to get the chilled bottle of wine. I leaned forward for him to get comfortable behind me. We ate in silence for a few moments while the events of earlier moved through my head.

"Baby, you do know that the guy from earlier meant no harm?"

"I don't know anything other than he did the opposite of what I told him."

I could feel the anger vibrating through his chest. After I had come back from the first round of snorkeling, I told the tour guide that I loved it. He asked if I wanted to go again. Jidenna said no. He was on edge about me going so deep in the water the first time. While I was still trying to get him to understand I was fine, and it was fun, the tour guide bumped into me by accident, and I landed back in the water. Jidenna dove in. That was completely unnecessary since I was a good swimmer. I didn't tell him that because by then he wasn't listening to anybody.

When we climbed back onto the boat, with fury blazing in his eyes, he had lifted the tour guide in the air. The guy was gasping for air with how tight Jidenna gripped his shirt.

"Didn't I tell you my wife was done?" he'd roared.

The other guide tried to calm Jidenna down, but he wasn't hearing anything. After calling his name and getting no response, I walked over and touched his arm. He let the guy go, but turned his anger on me, berating me for putting myself in harm's way. The only reason I didn't argue back was I saw real fear in his eyes. Something I had never seen before.

"I love you almost to the point of insanity. The safety of you and my daughter will always come first. Anything or anybody that threatens that will get cut down without questions." A beat passed between us. "We watched two days ago as a man tried to help his girl who had swallowed too much of that ocean water and was choking. However, your eyes lit up when you talked about diving, and I wasn't going to deprive you of the experience, or myself of your smile. But when I said it was enough, I meant it."

Wanting to change the tone of the evening, I changed the subject. "I can confidently say you've given me the experience of a lifetime. Thank you."

"You're welcome, but our lifetime isn't over yet. I wanna

thank you though." He chuckled. "For allowing me to spoil you without giving me too much hassle. I know your always-in-control self was fretting at the knees not knowing where we were going or what you were going to wear when we got there."

I smiled. Part of my annoyance on the trip over was he told me to get on the plane without so much as a packed bag. When we arrived, I suddenly had a bag. From dresses, shorts, jeans, shoes, lounge wear, swimming suits, my hair products to my crossbody—everything was in it. All fit perfectly.

"I'm still amazed at how you matched everything perfectly and my size too."

"Didn't you say something about attention to detail? What's mine, I study. Ain't nobody out there can tell me a thing about mine."

I grunted.

"I told Ci what I wanted. Color, size, and style. She did the shopping."

"I hope Ciara is on your payroll."

Ciara was Arinze's assistant, but the way Cheta and my husband acted, she worked for all three of them.

He snorted. "She gets compensated."

"Well, you did good, baby. I enjoyed my princess treatment."

"I aim to please."

As though on cue, "My Everything" by Sauti Sol ft. India Arie began to float through the villa. I stood, dragging my husband to his feet.

"Come on, baby, dance with me."

With his arms around my waist and mine around his neck, we stared into each other's eyes. Our love blazed through as I sang the lyrics of the song to my husband.

Sometime during the night, I woke to the sound of Jidenna murmuring. It almost sounded like he was admonishing himself. His body shook as he sat at the edge of the bed, his face buried in his hands. My eyes shifted to the clock on the dresser. It was a little after four a.m. Clearing the fog in my head, I pulled myself up, securing the sheet across my chest. I tried to recollect what happened last night. Other than us dancing, eating and a passionate love making session, I had nothing.

"Baby, what's wrong?" I asked, my voice soft and hushed.

He looked over his shoulder toward me, but didn't connect with my eyes. He hesitated, as if he couldn't find the words to explain, before finally speaking. "I'mma need you to get on birth control."

The words knocked the wind out of me. I wasn't sure I heard them the first time. I couldn't have. I swallowed the lump in my throat. "What?"

He stood. I stared at him, struggling to recognize the man I went to bed with.

"I don't want any more kids."

"Wait. What?" I grabbed the sheet and wrapped it around my naked body. I turned on the lamp. "What happened?" I took a step toward him, but he moved back. This was so left field that I struggled to find my bearings. "Let's talk about this."

He ran his hands over his hair, his face contorted in grief, anguish, and pain. I could feel my own tears beginning to well up in my eyes. I was shocked that he would even suggest such a thing, after all the conversations we'd had about starting a family.

"I can't believe you would even suggest such a thing," I said, my voice rising. "We've discussed having children, and now you're telling me you don't want to?"

"You discussed, I listened. But now I'm discussing, and you listen. I don't want any more kids." He looked away, unable to meet my gaze.

My body heated with rage. Thoughts of Caleb trying to control me by telling me what to do came flooding back in my memory. "If you don't want kids, why don't you get a vasectomy?"

This man laughed in my face as he pulled on his pants. The

more I thought about it, the more I realized I couldn't remember a time he released in me other than last night. I wasn't ovulating, but he didn't know that. Was the fact that he could have impregnated me so hard for him to accept? How could he love me but not want to have a baby with me?

I took a breath. This was madness. I loved Uju, but I wanted to have children of my own. Uju… Was this about her mother?

"Let's talk about this. Tell me what has you so rattled?" I asked, softly.

His eyes met mine and I thought I was getting through to him. But then, he said something that made my heart drop. "There's nothing to talk about. The deal was I save your family's name and you mother my child. Nowhere in our negotiation did it say we'll add any additional children." He pulled on his shirt and headed for the terrace that led to the beach.

"Where are you going?"

"I'll be back."

I plopped down on the bed and the levee broke. Tears streamed down my face. My head ached from the whiplash I got from his sudden mood change and this conversation. I wanted to follow him and get to the bottom of this. I knew without a doubt he loved me, but I could already feel the distance between us. I wanted to tell myself that this was all a bad dream, but my brain couldn't conjure up that tale. There was so much conviction in his voice. If his mission was to break me, I had no defense against the onslaught of pain he had inflicted. My walls were completely down with him. Every word he spoke was a shard of glass that ripped apart my soul. He deserved a medal for the way he had just smashed me to pieces.

13

JIDENNA

I messed up. Royally. I tried. I really did. But loving another woman unleashed a dark rush of emotions that I had evaded for nine long years. For nine years, my daughter, traveling around the world making a name for myself, satisfying my needs with nameless faces, had all been buffers from the feelings of powerlessness that now threatened to overwhelm me. All my efforts to avoid confronting the fear and helplessness in my life were futile.

Three months ago, everything came crashing down because of my stupidity and arrogance, destroying the happiness I had built, and I had no clue as to how to put it all back together.

"Nna, I'm done." Cheta got off the bench press he was on, his voice a tad higher than necessary. He strolled to the small fridge in the corner where Arinze stored Gatorade, various energy drinks and water.

I shook my head, wishing he was the punching bag before me. Since Cheta and I had very different personalities, we rubbed each other the wrong way often. That was my brother ten toes down, but sometimes I wished he'd tone it down a bit.

He unscrewed the cap of a Gatorade and took a long gulp. "Just because you're chasing a serotonin high, doesn't mean we all gotta suffer. My wife is willing and able to give me mine in measured doses."

I glared at him. A while ago, he'd given me a silly speech about how my foul attitude was a result of insufficient serotonin release. He went on to explain that the orgasm-like high the hormone emitted could also be attained from exercising. At the end of his speech, I was mad at the five minutes of my life I couldn't get back after listening to him. Just as I was now.

"Will you please be quiet?"

It was too late because his rant got Arinze's attention who removed the earbud from his other ear and turned off the tread-mill. "What is he talking about?"

My eyes shot up to Cheta who shrugged and began stuffing his things into his bag. July sped into October, and over the past several weeks, we had met at Arinze's house in his home gym to work out. It was something we all used to do when we were single, and we started back up. For me, it was for selfish reasons only. My wife was not messing with me on any level, and I needed to get away from her before I locked her in a room and begged her to talk to me.

For the first couple of weeks after we returned from Seychelles, she carried on as though I wasn't in the house. If she wasn't a dancer, acting was definitely her calling. Because in all the chaos, Uju didn't suspect a thing. I respected Zola for that. When Uju was out of the room or went down for the night, she turned into a whole different human being and made no secret that I was on her kill list. She joked that I could keep a grudge, but nobody could come close to her. She was classy with it too. That there had me ready to pull my hair out. I tried to apologize for speaking to her the way I did. That stuff fell on deaf ears. She wanted to discuss it and I couldn't. So, we were in a standoff.

One day, I got back from dropping Uju off with Reign who'd asked for her for the weekend. Zola had moved herself into the guest room. After pleading nicely that she let me in and getting no response, I took the door off the hinges. That weekend, flashes of the movie where Michael Douglas and Kathleen Turner fought to the death in a divorce battle flooded through my brain. My wife begged me to leave her alone for her own sanity. Her tears cracked my heart and I felt like crap. I moved her back to our room, took the guestroom and thus my travels restarted. I needed her and Uju comfortable and just like I told her, anything that threatened her well-being was going to get cut down. Now, that was me.

"Oh, you didn't tell him," Cheta asked, interrupting the silence.

My eyes met Arinze's for a second before I started undoing the wraps on my hands. I regretted even telling Cheta, and if he hadn't caught me at a moment of vulnerability, I wouldn't have.

My cousin had to make an appearance at a club and wanted me to go with him. That was when Zola told me that she was closed for "business." I was in my feelings and told my cousin I didn't want to be around any woman but mine. I knew he wouldn't cheat on Reign, but the booth we'd be in came with women, and my cousin was a magnet for the press and blogs that trolled. After he kept pressing me, I allowed my home situation to slip and regretted it immediately. I'm surprised it took him this long to say something.

"No, I didn't, but I know your big mouth will."

"I'm here to serve." Cheta saluted me then turned to Arinze who had moved closer to us. "This *anu nkpam* told Teach that she should get on birth control because he didn't want to have kids. And as my sis should, she decided to withhold the goodies from him. He's backed up for months."

My frustration got the best of me, and I charged toward him, but Arinze got in the middle of us before my fist could connect with his face.

"Nze, leave him. Let me drop him real quick. Don't be mad at me because you messed up the second chance God gave you."

"C, stop it."

"Nah, Nze. This fool has lost his mind coming at me. I've been with him every step of the way for weeks. Taking Ju when I can so he can fix his mess. I've said nothing. But now he thinks he can beat me?"

"Like when you had a problem with Rei, we didn't rally around you," I roared.

"Let's get it right. Y'all came over there on some Dr. Phil trip. I never called you—"

Arinze turned to him. "Because that's what family does. We show up!"

"And that's the only reason I haven't walked out that door. But sometimes you gotta knock *family* out."

"Both of you calm down!" Arinze roared.

We stewed in heated silence for a few moments. My chest heaved, the rage in me gnawing for a release. Arinze's voice sliced the charged atmosphere.

"Nna, I had scars from Chantel, Cheta had them from Finley, but when you find something good, you secure it. If you keep holding on to the past, your hands won't be free to grab the good," he said.

"You have a woman who loves you, your daughter, will go to war for you, and you don't want to give her the one thing she wants because you're afraid she might die? How do you think that will work out in the long run?" Cheta asked.

I began to pace. They both made it sound so simple. I was the one that lived with the dark shadows lurking in the corners of my mind. Rattled at the slightest hint of uncertainty. I was the one that heard the echoes in my heart reminding me of how far I could sink if anything went wrong. The ache in my heart and the knot in my stomach weighed me down when my mind traveled to that hospital corridor. Here one moment, gone the next. There would be no way for me to predict every situation with my wife, but I refused to contribute to one which I had already experienced its possible outcome.

"Don't you think I want to give my wife what she desires? Ever since we've had this rift between us, I don't get to see her smile. One that really comes from her heart and not those fake grins she plasters on. My existence is gloomy without it!" I rubbed the back of my neck and took a breath. "But the thought of anything going wrong paralyzes me. I should've left her alone. But me without her is no longer an option."

"Have you told her that? This…what you just told us."

I glanced at Arinze and shook my head before continuing my pace.

"How do I tell her I can't give her what she wants because I… me, the one who is supposed to protect her, is a freaking coward?"

"That's that ego. It will mess you up every time." Cheta added. His tone was calmer. "If you can't be vulnerable with your wife, y'all got bigger problems." He stood. "I'm out though. I gotta take Rei to the airport later. She's headed to DC for a conference. And I wanna get some time in before she leaves."

He dapped Arinze, but pulled me in for a hug and whispered, "Eno gave you the best gift ever, but ain't no way she would want you to be a prisoner to the past." He patted my back and left.

I had to move too. I stuffed my bag with my items, zipped it and hung it across my body. I could feel Arinze's eyes on me. I was all talked out. My house was empty and although I dreaded being there alone, I could use the rest from all the traveling I had done in the last three weeks. Zola was in Luxe Noir helping her mother with a community event she was hosting. Uju, who was on fall break was with her aunt who now lived in Dallas.

"What Nze? I can feel you staring at me. Speak your mind."

"Stop making God in your own image."

"What?"

"His power is limitless and sovereign. No matter how much power you think you have, when it comes down to it, God is in control of it all. Everything in life is temporary, so find the courage to enjoy what you got while you can."

I had no response for that, so I nodded. We all took our faith seriously. Church, charity, and we were also in our Bible when we could be. At least that was the case for me. But we didn't preach to each other. I needed to find out what Jasmine was doing to my cousin.

Raven leaned back in her chair and crossed her legs, then uncrossed them before leaning forward, her cleavage on display. She was playing games I didn't have the time for. When she entered my office about half an hour ago under the guise of straightening out the final details for an event that wasn't happening for another month, I knew she was up to no good. What she was talking about could have been handled over the phone. What was it about becoming more desirable when people found out you had a spouse?

She stood and walked over to me. I shot to my feet because the look in her eyes was giving sneaky and I was already in enough hot water at home and couldn't add any misunderstandings to the mix.

She stopped at the side of the desk and slightly leaned over to the pictures spewed across it. "I still think we should go with the other guy. Mansa has been tardy in responding to emails, turning in paperwork, and sending over his requirements. This is showcasing the Black experience and I want nothing about it to be sloppy."

I agreed with her, but once again, we could've discussed this over the phone. I was the contact in charge of the African representatives for the AfroFusion ArtFest three-day event. The aim was to show various artists from the north, south, east, and west of Africa. Since I was local, I would headline the African section, then introduce these other artists from the continent. We had other Black artists from the Caribbean, Europe, and other parts of the African Diaspora there too.

Mansa was the artist we chose from East Africa. He was a very brilliant artist, but something was going on with him because the enthusiasm he showed during the initial stages of contact had waned considerably. The last straw for Raven was his delay in giving transportation details for his display pieces. Again, I understood all of this, but Zola asked me to pick up Uju today and if I didn't get out of here soon, my wife would for sure have my behind.

A week had gone by since my cousins and I had our moment in Arinze's gym. Something happened when my wife was in Luxe, because when she got back, her ignore game strengthened. I could barely keep up with her. She was always busy. I know she was focused on the dance competition her senior class qualified for. They had gotten to the finals, and I had witnessed firsthand how focused and disciplined she could be when it was "go" time. That, planning our wedding reception in Luxe, and Uju had all her attention. When I tried to talk to her, she shut me down. Since this was all my doing, against my primal nature to demand my way, I backed down. She deserved whatever she asked for.

"Mr. Kalu, did you hear what I said?" Raven said, placing her hand on top of mine.

I retrieved my hand, letting hers drop. "I'm good with whoever you wanna go with, Ms. Collins." I placed my hands in my pockets. "Both of them are stand up guys. I understand your concerns about Mansa, so I'll reach out to him."

She nodded and began closing the files she brought over. The wedding reception for Zola and I was set before we traveled to Nigeria. The event, which was taking place in two days, was supposed to be an intimate affair at the Westbrook's beach house. With the number of times Zola's mom called asking one question or the other, I was questioning what intimate meant. While in Enugu, my parents prayed for us and blessed our union, so they wouldn't be there. My side of the family would comprise of, my cousins and their wives, Adaugo, Arinze's sister, who was flying in from Canada with her family, and Onyi.

How messed up was it that our celebration of love was going to be shrouded by my wife and I beefing. I picked up my jacket, but was startled by a hand slowly making its way up my arm. Other than a handshake, Raven had never touched me before. Between being startled and honing in on what she was saying, I froze.

"Are you okay? You seemed distracted," she purred.

My eyes went to her hand then traveled to her eyes. There was concern etched in her expression, but she ignored the look of discomfort in mine and kept her hand in place. I lifted my hand to hers when my door opened.

I had to have the worst luck in the world because my wife paused and took in the scene. Raven dropped her hand, but the speed at which she did it gave off vibes of guilt.

Zola's eyes shot daggers at me, and I knew for sure she was cussing me out in her head. The woman my wife was though, she would never allow those words leave her mouth. In her anger, she was still the most gorgeous woman I'd ever seen. Nobody touched her on any day.

"Hi, Zola," Raven said, shoving the files into her portfolio.

"Mrs. Kalu," Zola corrected without sparing her a glance. Her eyes remained on me, and I assimilated each emotion that danced in them. The one that gutted me was disappointment. "I've been trying to reach you."

I patted myself down, searching for my phone. My eyes roamed the space, then I saw it on the back display cabinet. I walked over to get it. When I turned around, my wife was gone. I gave Raven an annoyed glance and hightailed it out of my office. When I got outside, my wife was entering her car. I jogged over and placed my hand on the car right as she started the engine. This woman didn't even glance my way. I knocked on the window.

"Zola, Roll this window down! Now!" I never used her name, so she knew I meant business.

It wouldn't be my wife if she didn't mean mug me first. "What?!"

"Calm that down. I had a presentation earlier at the college and I turned off my phone. Not too long after I got back, Raven entered my office and so I didn't turn it back on."

"You have a wife and a kid. Your phone should never be off," she snapped.

"Don't come at me like I don't know that! You've never had a problem reaching me before," I seethed.

"There's always a first time for everything."

I hung my head and exhaled my exhaustion. I started us on this path, but I desperately needed to end it. I needed us back on the same page. "I'm tired of fighting, baby. I'm sorry."

She rolled her eyes, but I ignored her and listened to what she was here for. She had been at an appointment downtown when her mother called in a panic about the reception. Something about seating. Instead of Friday as originally planned, my wife decided to leave for Luxe this afternoon, taking Uju with her. She was calling me to let me know the change of plans. Who was I to tell her not to go? Even though I didn't like the fact that I'd be alone in the house again.

I leaned in and planted a kiss against her temple. "I love you. Be safe. Call me when you take off and when you get there."

"Will do."

She was about to wind up the window when I stopped her. "Don't ever let another woman see you sweat when it comes to me. I am yours, completely."

She sucked her teeth. "I didn't give her a second glance."

"You left her in the office with me. That speaks volumes."

"No, what speaks volumes is her leaned at the side of your desk with her hand on your shoulder." She wound up the window and backed out of the parking space. I watched her until she was out of the complex before I turned and headed back into the building. I needed to do something I should've done several minutes ago…kick Raven out.

Our guests had been celebrating for hours at the Westbrook beach home. The venue resembled a princess wedding in one of those princess movies that my daughter watched. Soft pink and champagne roses decorated the tents made up of soft white linens and fairy lights. The guest tables were decorated with crystal glasses and silverware, accompanied by fresh flowers and seashells as centerpieces.

Uniformed servers made sure drinks and food flowed nonstop. A variety of seafood dishes, such as shrimp cocktails, seared scallops, and grilled fish were served. I could smell the savory aromas from the cuisine over the ocean breeze. The sound of the waves lapping against the shore added a calming sound-track to the celebration. I had to give it to Zola's mom. That woman threw a mean party. Everything was perfect. Except…

She wouldn't even look at me.

My freaking wife wouldn't even look at me.

We were currently on the dance floor surrounded by friends and family. When Zola first appeared, my breath stilled. She was so beautiful. Her deep brown skin glowed in the delicate, one-shoulder, cream dress she wore. Her hair was styled on top of her head with some loose tresses framing her face. Her perfume wafted up my nostrils as I held her close. I was lost in her beauty. To everyone else we were fine. Some of her friends praised us all night, calling us couple goals. If only they knew. Swaying to our song with one arm around her waist, I lifted her face that was rested on my chest. "*Ola m*, look at me. Please," I whispered.

"Please don't. This is not the time or the place," she whispered back.

I had never been deprived of anything in my life. At least not since I became an adult. Since I got in yesterday, I'd been trying to get her alone, but every time I turned around, she was being cornered into one event or the other. I almost let her mother know Zola wasn't a bride. She was my wife, and this was just a reception. Now though, I was sick of it.

"Do you think I care about these people? I've been trying to talk to my wife, but she avoids me at every turn."

"Like you did her?" She raised her brow.

That was it!

I grabbed her hand and pulled her away from the dance floor. In the background, I could hear Arinze whisper my name. He must have seen my expression. Her mother who was beside us let out a gasp at the sudden movement. I was tunnel visioned, but from my peripheral I saw her brother, Jeremiah, walk towards us.

"Hey! Kalu, watch how you drag my sister."

I glanced over at Zola and her eyes pleaded for me to keep moving, so I did. Until her brother spoke again.

"Don't you—"

I was about to respond to him when I heard Cheta speak. "Jeremiah, step back man, that's that man's wife. She's good."

Without giving either of them a glance, I walked in the house, focused on finding an empty room. We entered her father's study and Zola snatched her hand from mine.

"Must we do this here? We have guests." She leaned on the oak desk.

I walked up to her and took her face in my hands. "I'm sorry for putting us on the path we've been on for the past couple of months. For not communicating and planting insecurities that is my job to make sure never gain root. I love you, baby."

"Why?"

After a long pause, I spent the next few minutes narrating to my wife the nightmare I had on the last night of our honeymoon. That night, after we talked and danced the night away, we went to bed. Our lovemaking that night was an experience I'd never felt. Our rhythm was passionate and intense—it was almost like a spiritual exchange of souls. Then, we went to sleep in each other's arms.

A few hours later I woke up with a jolt covered in sweat. My heart thumped in my chest, my eyes blurred as my head pounded and blood rushed to my ears. The metallic smell of the hospital walls, the blaring sound of the monitors, doctors and nurses rushing to Eno's bed while I fought against security trying to get me out of the room… Everything was so vivid like I was back in that hospital room nine years ago.

But it wasn't Eno in the room. It was Zola.

I looked over and my wife slept so peacefully, but my heart wouldn't stop thumping. Then I realized that I might have gotten her pregnant that night. I know it didn't make sense, but asking her to get on birth control was all I had.

I buried my head in the crook of my wife's shoulder. "You probably think I'm a coward."

Zola lifted my head. "I'm sorry you had to go through that alone. You're not a coward because you feel what you feel. You were selfish when you refused to shed your layers for the one you claim to love. If you don't trust me with you, then what are we doing? Because I trust you with every fiber of mine, but I refuse to be with someone who won't do the same for me." Her expression was unreadable. She pulled away from me and took a step back, her hand slipping from mine.

"Be patient with me."

I knew I had no right to ask her for anything. I wasn't stupid. I saw how my words crushed her that day and my actions ever since. But she was all I had, and I would fight for us with everything at my disposal.

14

ZOLA

It was a couple of weeks later, mid-Tuesday morning when I inhaled deeply and stepped onto the dance floor of Leap & Twirl. The infectious enthusiasm of my senior students gave me an unexplainable high. The sweat-and-perfume scent saturated the air, reminding me of all the hard work we'd done to get to the finals. My smile was wide and confident, mirroring the feelings I had inside. After our routine, start of session prayer, everyone took their positions. The beginning beat of "Remember the Time" by Michael Jackson began to play. I rotated my neck and let the melody take me away. In this space and at this time, all my problems took a backseat as I took in a breath, prepared to do what I knew without a doubt I was created for.

Dance.

My movements were fluid and graceful as I demonstrated the new routine. My students followed my every step, their eyes on me with genuine interest. There was charged energy in the room.

"Let's break it down," I said calmly, but firmly. "Start with the footwork."

The determination in their faces showed they were

committed to learning each part of the choreography. I offered feedback and guidance as we practiced, making sure each student was operating at their highest potential. Seeing them like this filled me with so much pride. It did something to me to know they trusted me with one of their most creative forms of expression.

For the next hour, we continued to practice until it was time for a break. As the girls filed out, Tessa popped her head in the studio. Waving her in, I picked up a towel and walked towards her.

"I would hug you, but you're sweaty. Only one person should enjoy touching your sweaty body."

I rolled my eyes. "Girl, be quiet. Head to the office. Let me talk to my new teacher."

"The new girl? Don't tell me she's in trouble already?"

I frowned at her. "No, she's not. I wanna make sure she's settling in okay. What's wrong with you?"

Minutes later, my eyes darted toward the timer on my laptop. I had a lunch date with Jasmine and Reign to go over Uju's birthday party plans on Saturday. I was the furthest one away and I hated being late.

"So y'all okay now?" Tessa asked as I went through the pictures on her phone. Right after my wedding reception, she traveled to Sint Maarten on a solo trip.

"'Cause when that man grabbed you off the dance floor, I was like Jeremiah – ready to fight."

I laughed. Jidenna was quite dramatic, but even on his worst day, he wouldn't harm me. I understood his frustration because I had been dodging him like a quarterback dodging a tackle. It was hard enough keeping my mother out of my business the weekend of the community event when she went on about how I wasn't behaving like a newlywed. I could divert her attention when I was solo, but that weekend at the reception, I knew I had to be extra covert. One thing my older sister told me when I was getting married the first time was to never share any disagreements my husband and I had with my mother. Unless it was abuse, keep it to yourself.

"Zee, when you and Caleb make up, which you most likely will, Mom will never forget how you hurt then. You've forgiven him because you love him. Mom, on the other hand, has no allegiance to that man, so there would be a rift there that you'd rather not deal with."

Although my mother could tell my husband loved me, she was antsy about our cultural difference. Even my trip to Nigeria had her on edge.

I pondered Tessa's question as I felt the burn of her stare. Were we good? I hadn't shared the reason my husband gave for his cold shoulder, but she did know of our issues. She was my best friend and I needed to talk. For the most part, I had my husband back. Truthfully, even when we were at odds, he never slacked as my man. The only thing that changed was the frequency of his travel, something I was also grateful for.

He dropped in to bring me lunch occasionally, made sure I never had to worry about my car being fueled or needing an oil change. He helped with the celebration the staff and students had to mark the ownership change. When he thought I was asleep, he would pray over me as he always did. He was so good at being a husband and a father that Uju didn't notice much. The only thing that was missing was how he touched, kissed, made love to me, and read to me every night. I missed the smoothness of his rasp as he read the latest mystery that was unfolding in the latest S.D Harris novel.

"I mean as good as we can be while ignoring the crux of the problem." I sighed.

"That's not healthy, sis."

"I know that. I miss my husband, but I'm at a total loss right now."

"Does he know you suffer from endometriosis?"

I stared at her, causing Tessa to lean back in her chair and frown. "Are you serious? Why?"

"We've not even been married a year. It's not something that's a dinner discussion. I mean, he has seen me maybe once or twice in severe pain. He thought it was a painful period." I shrugged. "Then the way he hovered, going on and on about my comfort, what I craved...it was too much. Plus, he got mad when I told him to go away." I giggled recollecting the specific day in question.

"Something's gotta give though..."

I took my hair out of its bun. "I know, but right now, I'm exhausted."

"Didn't y'all discuss kids before marriage?"

"No. First, we were in such a hurry, and we weren't even on that kind of time then. Then, when we did talk about children..." I shook my head. "He was right...I talked, and he listened. He didn't add anything. I didn't think it was an issue because what Nigerian man doesn't want children?"

Tessa laughed and I saw nothing funny in the situation. "Apparently yours."

Frustration settled in my stomach. Standing, I began gathering my things. I needed to get home and freshen up before heading back out. "Now I'm talking crazy. I need to get going."

"Not crazy. You're understandably stressed, but I promise everything will work itself out. Jidenna loves you."

"Our love isn't in question."

"What's your plan?"

After a long, drawn-out grunt, I placed my bag on my shoulder. "Continue to love him where he is, but set boundaries for myself. That's all I got."

I rounded the desk and Tessa pulled me to her. After telling me she loved me, she picked up her purse. She'd flown in two days ago for a meeting with her counterparts at Piedmont Hospital.

"All right, I got a plane to catch. Besides, you have a lunch date with your new best friends. Hmmm… Don't be telling them everything you tell me, either."

"I wouldn't dream of it."

We both laughed and walked out of my office. After I gave some last-minute instructions, we left the studio, each of us going our separate ways.

Uju's tenth birthday celebration was in full swing. The backyard had been converted into the magical setting of the Disney movie, *The Princess and the Frog*, complete with the iconic wrought iron balconies and pastel-colored buildings that lined the streets. Her uncle, Arinze, had pulled some serious strings and the mini sound stages had been turned into the bustling French Quarter, complete with its vibrant jazz clubs and actors cosplaying as colorful street performers. Twinkling lights and colorful balloons adorned every corner.

The music stopped and a hush fell over our thirty something guests. My eyes went to Uju's, who turned her head to find me. Her wide smile of anticipation captured my heart. I leaned into her dad who held me from behind. I could feel a tear form in the corner of my eye and quickly thumbed it away. This look on my daughter's face was one I also wanted to see on my future children's faces. A dream I felt slipping further into the abyss with each passing day.

Suddenly, actors dressed as the frog version of Princess Tiana and Prince Naveen appeared on the makeshift stage we'd set up. The deafening sounds of screaming kids filled the atmosphere. The performers began reenacting the scene where the frogs turn back into humans. After watching them for a few minutes, a satisfied grin spread across my face. Jidenna kissed the crook of my neck.

"Thank you, baby."

I turned to look up at him. "I'll be back. Let me go check on the cake."

"Didn't you hire people for that?"

"I did, but I still need to make sure everything is going according to plan."

He nodded and I walked through the sliding patio doors. He was right. I hired very efficient people, however, I needed to get away from him for a few moments. The boundaries I set worked except when we had family and friends around. Right now, the house was filled with them, and I needed a little breather.

After popping into the kitchen to ensure the two-tier, green and gold chocolate cake would make its appearance on schedule, I took the stairs, two at a time to my bedroom. Walking into the room, I plopped down on the bed. Cupping my face in my hands, I drew in a long, deep breath.

In a couple of days, Jidenna would leave for L.A. for a three-day weekend event with him as the keynote speaker. I couldn't imagine my life without Uju in it. Not anymore. But when he got back, we needed to have a conversation. There was no way I was living the rest of my life with this cloud over us.

"I can't do this," I muttered.

"You can't do what?"

I looked up and Jasmine and Reign walked in. Jasmine had that pregnancy glow and she looked so adorable. She waddled toward the bed while Reign propped herself up against the dresser.

"We were worried, knocked, and you didn't answer, so we came in," Reign summarized. She was so much like her husband that it was annoying sometimes.

"What's wrong? And don't give us that polished answer you gave a few days ago," Jasmine said.

"No matter what y'all think, you and your hubby are not fooling anyone." Reign walked toward me and leaned against the bed post. "I thought we agreed to be there for each other? Not that I wanna hear everything y'all got going on, 'cause I got my own Kalu man to deal with but…"

"You've not been yourself. Maybe we can help."

It had to be the sincerity in Jasmine's tone that opened my tear ducts because before I could stop them, the tears flowed. I could see the surprise in their eyes when I told them how he didn't contact me after the Morehouse event. Then the real story behind our marriage. I ended the story with how we'd not being getting along for the past four and a half months because he was allowing his past to complicate our future.

Apart from their initial surprise about him ghosting me, they didn't seem moved by our union starting off as a sham. Instead, they looked at each other and laughed.

Annoyed, I stood. "If you wanted a comedy show, you could've stayed downstairs."

"Girl, chill out. We're laughing because both of us started off as shams too," Reign said.

"Now, Grandma Kalu is my girl, but I couldn't believe she was actually auditioning women for her grandson," Jasmine said.

She began giving me details of how she and Arinze met in Montego Bay. Then months later, reconnected through a dating agency when he wanted to "rent a bae" to convince his grandma he had his relationship covered.

"That woman is something else." Reign chuckled. "My Che bear was under the same kind of pressure, but my silly behind walked right into becoming his makeshift fiancée," Reign said.

"Don't let that man hear you call him that," Jasmine said.

I saw the articles and read the blogs dragging Reign and Cheta for filth after a recording of them in a compromising posi-tion leaked. I wasn't aware though, of the background that pushed them into their engagement.

"What we're trying to say is that you may have started off as a ploy…we did too. But believe me, everything will be fine. That man isn't letting you go, and we know how he feels about his *Ola*."

Jasmine winked at me, and I took a breath. Allowing their words to sink in, I exhaled and stood. Both ladies drew me in for a hug. Everyone kept saying it would be fine. I wanted to believe them, but I had no idea how or when.

Two days later, I was overwhelmed by an intense pain under my right rib. I tried to pray for the agony to go away, but neither that nor my medication was working. While struggling to contain my brokenness, I noticed Uju on the corner of the couch. The look in her eyes was one of terror.

With her dad out of town, we'd planned a girls night in. A day full of in-home pampering: manicure and pedicure, massages, and facials. While enjoying her choice of movies, we'd planned to heat up the leftovers the private chef prepared the day before.

All those plans evaporated in the wee hours of the morning when I went to pee, and pain shot up through my spine. My baby and I were home alone, and I didn't wanna call anyone over because I really thought I could push through it.

Her intense gaze penetrated me and sent chills down my spine. Feeling vulnerable and weak, but fiercely protective, I reached out for her. She moved closer to me.

"Mummy Zola, I'm scared. You've been crying."

"I'm fine, baby. I have a little pain that will soon go away. Can you go upstairs and get my phone?"

Uju nodded and ran up the stairs. I didn't have the strength to caution her about running up the stairs as I normally would have. As time went by, I was coming to terms with the fact that I might have to go to the hospital. I wanted my phone nearby to make a few calls. I wasn't looking forward to that, neither was I looking forward to having medical professionals make light of my situation.

"I don't know what's wrong with her, but she has been crying and holding her stomach. My daddy is not here."

"Uju, who's on the phone?"

She walked closer to me, tears in her eyes. With the little energy I had, I pulled myself into a seating position. Uju handed me her phone and it was Arinze. I answered the questions he had. His tone moved from concern for me, to annoyance at why I didn't call someone sooner, before landing on irritation at my stubbornness. When he was satisfied with my answers, we hung up the phone. I wanted to question why Uju called her uncle, but she was worried enough. She found her place on the floor at the end of the sofa while I shut my eyes once again, longing for comfort.

A few hours later, my longing was fulfilled when the pain medication settled in my veins.

"Nna, stop asking me questions I don't have the answer to. When you get here, ask them. All I know is she's no longer in pain and resting. Uju is with Jas. How much longer?"

My eyelids fluttered at Arinze's voice. The last thing I remembered was him entering our home and asking if I could walk. I vaguely remembered taking too long to answer then being swept off my feet and deposited in his truck. As we drove to the hospital, he called Jidenna and put him on speaker. I could hear the panic in his voice, but I didn't have the energy to assuage his fears.

When we got to the hospital, Arinze demanded I was given a private room, then shortly after, samples were taken for tests.

"How you feeling, Zee?"

"I'm okay, thank you," I whispered.

"We're family." He paused. "I'mma go down to the cafeteria for some coffee. You want something?"

"No." He gave me a head nod and began to leave. "Arinze, I know we're family, but I'm sorry to have put you out."

He smiled. "I'm good, but be ready to square up with Jas because she says ain't no way you were in pain for hours and didn't call her or Reign." He grinned and walked out of the door.

Several hours later, Jidenna squeezed my hand and stared into my eyes. His eyes misted and my heart broke for him. I couldn't imagine what the last few hours had done to him. It was as though he had aged on the flight back from L.A. According to him, he was toward the end of his keynote speech when Arinze's 911 text came through. In less than fifteen minutes, he was packed and chartered a private jet.

"Please, don't scare me like this again. The whole way here, I had an outer body experience." A weary smile spread across his face. "I need to apologize to the lady at the front desk."

"Oh gosh. What did you do?" My husband arrived a few minutes ago and we were currently waiting on the doctor who was consulting with my gynecologist.

"I kept telling her I was here to see my wife. She kept saying her husband was already in here. I had a few choice words for her."

I groaned. "The quiet ones really are the worst."

"Only when it comes to my family." He leaned and planted a kiss on my forehead.

It had been too long since he had given me a real kiss. Moments later, there was a knock on the door and the doctor walked in. The older Black man had an unreadable expression on his face. After introducing himself to Jidenna, he asked if I was okay with him sharing information in front of my husband. Jidenna's face contorted and he opened his mouth to respond, but I squeezed his hand cutting his tantrum off.

"Okay, Ms. Westbrook, the—"

"Mrs. Kalu," Jidenna corrected.

"Mrs. Kalu, the tests came back, and the scarring has returned…but not much."

"Scarring? Where?" Jidenna asked. His eyes darted from the doctor to me before resting on the doctor.

For the few minutes that followed, the doctor gave my husband an endometriosis-for-beginner's summary. As he ran down the symptoms, the risk factors, and steps that could be taken to reduce and in rare cases, eliminate the symptoms, I sensed Jidenna's anger. His eyes kept moving from the doctor to me before he finally hung his head.

"After consulting with your doctor, we agreed it's not severe enough to require surgery. Instead, we recommend a stricter diet and continued pain management."

After answering a few more questions, we thanked the doctor, and he made his way to the door. I shifted under my husband's gaze. "Doctor, when can I take her home?"

"I'll send the nurse in to get her vitals. If all is well, I'll write up the discharge papers and you guys can be on your way." He looked at the clipboard in his hand before raising his eyes. "Make an appointment to see your gynecologist next week."

After we thanked him once again, he continued to the door before abruptly turning to us. "She did say to remind you that if you're still intent on having children, the window is closing." After dropping that bombshell, he left the room.

Later that night, while propped up against the headboard, my eyes followed my husband's movements. Just out the shower, using a towel to cover his lower half, he stepped over to the dresser to moisturize his skin before slipping into the roomy, walk-in closet. I folded my arms and took a deep breath. It was a little after midnight and we'd been back from the hospital for about an hour. Since then, my husband hadn't said one word to me. He had a tight jaw and deep frown lines as he had slowly washed me from head to toe, lotioned and put on my sleepwear before securing my silk bonnet.

He disappeared to the kitchen for a few minutes before returning with a sandwich, some tea, and a bottle of water. After making sure I ate and took my medication, he walked into the bathroom to take a shower. Appearing a few minutes later in a white tee and his boxers, he sat at the edge of the bed with his back toward me. The silence in the room was deafening and suffocating. The built-up tension in me was on the verge of explosion. I mustered up the courage to break the ice.

Finally, I cleared my throat and spoke up, "Are you gonna keep ignoring me, or tell me what's you're thinking?"

He slowly turned around, his eyes blazing with anger. "We've been married seven months. What I'm thinking is how you kept this from me all this time. Why didn't I notice? How can you be dealing with this and not tell me?"

"The same way you were dealing with your stuff and not telling me."

"That's different!" He stood and leaned against the post of the bed.

"Why? Because yours is mental and mine is physical? A struggle is a struggle, baby. We're supposed to be partners, but you changed that. Your fear is one thing, but keeping it from me was another thing entirely."

"Is this why you want to have a child?"

"Pregnancy can help, but it's not a guarantee, so no. I've always wanted children because I've wanted to be a mother ever since I can remember." I exhaled. "I want to have children *now*, because despite all the hormonal therapy and surgeries I've had, there's still a chance of infertility."

"So why didn't you tell me that?"

"For someone who was bent on keeping his stuff to himself, you sure are mad about being kept in the dark."

"Zola, cut it out! I've apologized. That still doesn't excuse you. So, you were going to settle for me saying I didn't want to have children?" He began to pace. "That tears me up with fury. How could you settle knowing I was working, unknowingly might I add, against your interest?"

"I wasn't settling. I did send you the text that we needed to talk."

"Only after I told you we had to fix our mess before the holidays." He stopped mid stride. "I can't believe you, woman."

I shrugged. "The pool guy was looking quite enticing. If it wasn't you, it would've—"

He paused. His fiery stare kept my chuckle in my throat. "Don't put that man's life in danger because you want to be funny." He took a few more steps before he stopped. "Let's have a baby then."

This time it was my turn to pin him with a heated gaze. "I don't want your little pity baby."

Jidenna got on the bed and crawled toward me. His face was near mine. "Nothing about my baby will be little or pitiful. Trust me."

I tried to push him back and crossed my arms. "Move, I'm serious. I don't want you to have a baby with me just to help me."

His brows dipped. "Why not? You've helped me since I met you. With my daughter, my family, how to become a better version of myself, showed me how to love again. Since the day you walked your pretty self in my office, you've been helping me. So, tell me again why I can't help you?"

"I want us to have children because you want to, not out of obligation."

"My hesitation was never about not having children with you. It was about the fear of an experience I know I'd die from if it happened to you." He leaned against the headboard and gathered me in his arms. "Right before our reception in Luxe, I had my first session with a therapist. I'm working on me because I won't walk this earth while you're unhappy. Then after what I saw and heard today, you really think I won't work my behind off to make sure I support and be there for you in every way possible? You're my wife and I love you. I want to see you happy and fulfilled."

I shifted my body and straddled him. His hand rested on my waist as our eyes remained locked in. His warm, brown eyes melted away my fears. I could trust him with my heart, body, and my future.

"I love you, too." Feeling my eyes tear up, I leaned in and

kissed my husband deeply, feeling a sense of hope and excitement for the future.

Jidenna's hand went around my neck, and he nipped my earlobe before whispering, "*Olaedo m*, when can we start practicing?"

I chuckled and collapsed into him, feeling the power of our love surging through me. Our happily ever after was a daily commitment I'd never stop fighting for.

THE END

EPILOGUE

Thirteen months later...

I stared at my reflection in the bedroom mirror and for the first time in months, I let myself exhale. Through my nose, I expelled worry and inhaled peace. The lives growing inside me were no longer just a concept, a potential, or a distant dream. For most of the last thirty-four weeks, a part of me was scared to accept them as tangible reality.

I cradled my stomach and hummed to the melody of "Lord Do It For Me" by Zacardi Cortez playing in the background. After three months without success in conceiving, then another three months of fertility treatments, I'd almost given up hope of having a baby. Those six months, I felt as though my dream would never be a reality. The song became my anthem after I heard it while aimlessly scrolling my Instagram feed after a crying session. It was one of those days I struggled to hold on to hope.

I smiled remembering the day Jidenna and I found out we

were pregnant. We couldn't contain ourselves, but decided to keep it between us. Then we found out we were having twins. The feelings of anxiety mixed with joy were a rocky terrain to navigate. Jidenna stopped traveling altogether and became my chauffeur. He didn't last on the job for more than a week because I fired him. He was not about to drive me crazy.

He was already bad before with his overprotectiveness, but he was a whole different beast when the doctor said I was high risk. The man didn't want me to do anything. I knew he was worried; my man was on high alert. He had really done his grief work, but I still understood his plight. When I told him his stress was rubbing off on me, he chilled a bit.

I felt a presence behind me, and I knew without looking that it was my husband. He tucked his chin in the crook of my neck and cradled my stomach. His touch was gentle and loving, providing the safety and protection I was used to.

"Hey, baby."

"*Ola m.*" He kissed my neck and stood to his full height. "You know you're so hardheaded. Why are you on your feet?"

I leaned into him, and our eyes connected through the mirror. "I've not been on my feet long. Don't start, please."

"You wanted this, and I made it happen. I promise, if I see you display any sign of discomfort...even once, I'm sending everybody home and you're coming right back to bed."

During our fifth month, we had a scare when I began spotting. After an overnight stay at the hospital, I was discharged with a clean bill of health. But my mind refused to agree with the doctor and so I held my breath. Afraid to breathe.

Subsequently, I refused a baby shower, barked at my husband when he returned home one day with a cute newborn set, and stopped the decoration of the nursery. My husband and daughter were walking on eggshells around me, but did as I asked.

Last week after Zuri, Tessa, Jasmine, and Reign arrived for an intervention, I talked to Jidenna, who gave me the line his therapist gave him.

"The wall you build to shut out pain also shuts out joy."

Since I'd waited so long to change my mind about having a shower, my girls were all busy, so my hubby came to the rescue. He hired an event planner who put together an intimate shower that was starting in an hour.

I smiled. "I hear you."

"I'm serious. You look beautiful by the way." He kissed the top of my head.

Since the event was taking place in a large, heated tent at the back of the house, I decided to go simple. I had on a green, flared, sweater dress with black leggings and my knotless braids were in a low ponytail.

"Thank you. You look good too, baby."

He held me for a moment, and I couldn't help but feel a deep love and connection to him resting in his embrace. We stood there together, enveloped in a blanket of silence, but were soon interrupted by a knock on the door.

Uju stuck her head in. "Mummy Zola, are you ready? Auntie Jas and Auntie Rei are here with my uncles."

"Ju, did you open the door without an adult?" I asked. My baby was growing, but she was not that grown.

She let out a heavy sigh like I was getting on her nerves. I narrowed my eyes at her, and she gave me a wide grin. After explaining it was Eva who opened the door, she disappeared. I turned to my husband who smirked.

"Nope. You created that. I'm not in it."

I swatted his shoulder. He had a point, but my girl wasn't that bad. She was smart, kept good grades and helped around the house. She was now in middle school and that preteen attitude kicked in sometimes. Her dad had no patience for it, so I ran interference. They still had their bond, but my husband was uneasy with her growing up on him.

A few hours later, I reentered the tent, back from my umpteenth bathroom break. The party was winding down, but no one seemed eager to leave. I stood at the entrance watching our family and close friends enjoy themselves. Our babies had so many gifts they really didn't need. Jidenna and I had bought everything. But our people were not hearing it.

My brothers sat in the corner with my husband and his cousins. They got along better now, and I was so happy about that. Tessa, Jasmine, and Reign were in another corner attending to the caterers. Zuri and her husband had to leave early as they were headed to join his parents in Cape Town for a family event. My parents had already set sail on a cruise when I decided I wanted to have a shower, so they weren't here. Zekia promised to fly in when I had the babies.

The beat to "2 Step" by Ed Sheeran ft. Lil Baby dropped and I smiled when my husband started searching for me. We had added the song to our growing playlist and danced to it often.

Reaching me, he stretched out his hand. "Two step with me, baby."

Placing my hand in his, he twirled me slowly before leaning my back against his chest.

"I'll step with you today, forever and always." I closed my eyes and allowed myself to be in that moment while hopeful for what the future had in store.

"Babe, are you still here? Go, we'll be fine."

My wife lay propped up against the headboard in our bedroom, her eyes drooping from exhaustion. I walked up to her and sat on the edge of the bed, pressing my forehead gently against hers.

"Are you sure?" I asked.

"Yes," she said. "Besides, my mom is in her room and Eva is

also here." There was a hint of sarcasm in her voice when she mentioned her mother.

"Be nice," I chided.

"I will," she grumbled.

Two weeks ago, my wife and I were playing Scrabble and I was eviscerating her with the number of points I was ahead. Then as she always did, she began to fuss that I was cheating, but this time her theatrics came with tears. When she looked down, I followed her line of sight and my eyes bugged. Her water had broken. Her wide eyes jolted me into action.

As we raced to the hospital, I called our families. I'd never prayed as hard as I did as my wife went through labor and delivery. It felt like my soul was leaving my body in panic. I'd practiced for the moment, but nothing compared to the real thing. However, my coping mechanisms kept me from losing my mind. Eva was the first to arrive, so I left Uju with her and went to be with my wife. Many tension-filled hours later, my kids graced this world with their presence.

I stared at the blessings God had given me. My beautiful wife, Ebube and Ebere, my newborn son and daughter who lay asleep in the bassinet next to the bed. My first born, Uju, who was also out for the count, occupied my side of the bed.

My family.

"Call me if you need anything. I should be back in a couple of hours," I said.

"I got this. Go."

"*Ola m*, I'm serious."

"We always need you, but we'll be fine. It's just a few hours." She yawned.

I cupped her face with both hands, capturing her eyes. "I wasn't looking for you when you walked into my life, but no version of me exists without you. Thank you for helping me start over. I love you, Zola Kalu."

My wife yawned and I couldn't even be mad at her. Despite

her mom, Eva, and I being at her beck and call, she insisted on doing as much as she could for the twins herself while still making sure Uju got the attention she was used to getting from her. Gently easing her into the bed, I pulled the covers up around her shoulders before pressing a kiss to her forehead.

"I love—" she yawned again. "I love you too," she finished sleepily.

We'd been home for a week and some change, and this was the first time I was leaving their side. Zola encouraged me to get some air, so I decided to see my cousins real quick. After planting a kiss on each of my kids' foreheads, I left the room.

Minutes later, I dapped Cheta as I entered his den.

"If it isn't the newest father in town," he hailed.

Arinze came around the corner and we dapped up. Cheta got us drinks and we all sat around his den, shooting the breeze for a while until I asked.

"C, are you going to join the club any time soon?"

Nze and Jas now had a ten-month-old daughter, Adanna. My niece stole her mother's whole face. The only thing she got from Arinze was his skin tone.

"Nope." Cheta shrugged. "Maybe in a year or two. *Asa m* and I still have places we want to travel and explore."

Despite their hectic schedules, he and Reign still found time for spontaneous travel. Even though he left the league after giving Atlanta another championship, the blogs invented new ways to use his name as click bait. But neither of them seemed bothered, and I admired them for it.

"Ask your cousin why he's over there pouting." Cheta laughed.

I turned my head to Arinze, and he really looked like he was about to slap someone.

"Nze, *o gini?*" I asked.

He glanced my way then returned his eyes to the muted movie on the screen.

"Jas finally set the date for a few weeks, so what's the issue?"

His delayed wedding ceremony was the only thing I thought of that had him vexed lately. After Jas had Adanna, she delayed the ceremony again. This time she wanted to lose weight. The only reason I knew that was because of my wife. Arinze didn't talk about it. Instead, he walked around mad. But then they gave out save the date cards, so we were getting ready for their destination wedding. They wanted to be married where they first met...Montego Bay.

"Yesterday, she started talking about how the wedding dress she ordered was messed up during shipping. To get another one will take several weeks." He threw the rest of his drink down his throat and leaned back in the recliner he was on. "I told her if she pushes this wedding again, I'm taking my daughter and we're going to live happily ever after without her."

Cheta and I shared a glance and let out a loud cackle. Nze was big mad. I and Cheta didn't see the big deal—they were already married. But the man wanted his wedding and Jas was treading on thin ice. Arinze was putty in his wife's hand, but he had extra base in his voice tonight. I'd have to put a bug in my wife's ear to feel Jas out.

Moments later, Arinze asked, "When is Aunty coming over?" He was referring to my mother while subtly shifting the attention away from himself.

I followed his lead. "Zola's mom is still here, so after she leaves."

In Igbo culture, it was more common for the mother of the new mother to come for *Ọmụgwọ* first. So, Zola's mom had been with us since we got back from the hospital. My wife's patience was wearing thin, so I didn't see that lasting too much longer.

Cheta stood and walked over to adjust his sound system. "Chai! I miss Papa o. Remember when he and Mama sat us down to threaten us about letting the Kalu bloodline die?"

We grunted then laughed. That seemed like a lifetime ago. Our grandfather passed away about nine months ago. The family took it hard, and our grandmother was understandably torn up about it. She was thankful though, as we were, that he got to see the three of us settle down with women we loved and who loved us back.

I checked the time. Our grandmother would still be awake, so I told Cheta to call her on WhatsApp video call. The three of us gathered by the ringing phone, just as we had done a few years back. She answered on the third ring. We greeted her, and she was happy to see us. Her smile these days was rare, so I was glad we could do that for her. We chatted a bit, then she asked about our families and prayed for us before we disconnected the call.

"Ojemba" by Phyno and Olamide began to play in the background, and I bopped my head to the melody.

"Turn that stuff up…that's the jam," Arinze said.

Cheta picked up the remote to increase the volume. The three of us swayed to the song by the Nigerian rappers who thanked God for how far they'd come, the blessing He'd bestowed on them and His continued protection. The song played in a loop as we talked, laughed, and shared stories. I was thankful for the bond we had, despite our different paths and pursuits. We were all we had in America, so family would always come first.

GLOSSARY

<u>Pidgin/Igbo Translations</u>

The Kalus are from Enugu State located in the South Eastern part of Nigeria. They're of the Igbo ethnicity. Below are translations (done to the best of my ability) to the languages I used in the story. I have this in the order in which they appear.

Nwa m: My child (Igbo)

O kwa: Also (Igbo)

E wo: Gosh (Igbo)

Omalicha: Beautiful woman (Igbo)

Chineke: God (Igbo)

Nne anyi ukwu: Big Mama (Igbo)

Ka chi fo: Goodnight (Igbo)

Abeg: Please o (Pidgin)

Obi m: My heart (Igbo)

O we ife ne me gi nisi: Is something wrong with your head or are you crazy? (Igbo)

Nwoke m puo ebe a: This man, get outta here (Igbo)

Olaedo m: My jewel (Igbo)

Ị na-anụ ihe m na-agwa gị?: Do you understand what I'm telling you? (Igbo)

anụla m: I understand (Igbo)

Ke kwanu: How are you? (Igbo)

Daalu Nne m: Thank you my daughter. (Igbo)

ịchafụ: Head tie for Igbos (Igbo)

anu n kpam: complete animal (Igbo)

Asa m: My beauty (Igbo)

Oga: Prefix that shows sign of respect. Like "sir" (Pidgin)

O gini? What is it? (Igbo)

Ọmụgwọ: The process of which a family member (normally the mother) takes care of a new mother and her baby, in a short period of time after childbirth. Normally the first forty days.

FINAL NOTE

Thank you for reading Jidenna & Zola's story. Please consider leaving a review/rating on the platform you purchased the book from. I greatly appreciate your honest feedback. They really go a long way. The number of reviews a book receives greatly improves its visibility.

If you liked this story, I trust you might like some of my other titles. But before we get to those, I'd love to stay connected. Never miss a sale, new release announcements, or freebies. You can ensure you're in the know by joining my mailing list.

Next up for the Kalu family is the Arinze & Jasmine wedding. RSVP here

SAVE THE DATE

The Wedding of

Jasmine Bowman
&
Arinze Kalu

Late Summer, 2023
Montego Bay

Exclusive ONLY to
Newsletter subscribers

ALSO BY UNOMA NWANKWOR

Stand Alone Books

An Unexpected Blessing

He Changed My Name

When You Let Go

Full Circle

The Ultimatum Series

The Christmas Ultimatum

The Final Ultimatum

Sons of Ishmael Series

A Scoop of Love

Anchored by Love

Mended with Love

Redeemed Through Love

Mixed Tidings

The Invisible Shackles Series

To Live Again,

To Breathe Again

The DuBois-Arazi Family Novels

A Promise Fulfilled

Destiny Fulfilled

The Billionaire Pact

Vegas Nights

Second Shot

Pretend Bae

Away To Africa

New Year's Kiss (Prequel)

Rent-A-Bae

His Makeshift Fiancée